NIGHTS REMEMBERED

Adell & Tom
Good neighbors

Bruce Collier

NIGHTS REMEMBERED

Bruce Collier

iUniverse, Inc.
New York Lincoln Shanghai

NIGHTS REMEMBERED

Copyright © 2005 by Bruce Collier

All rights reserved. No part of this book may be used or reproduced by any means, graphic, electronic, or mechanical, including photocopying, recording, taping or by any information storage retrieval system without the written permission of the publisher except in the case of brief quotations embodied in critical articles and reviews.

iUniverse books may be ordered through booksellers or by contacting:

iUniverse
2021 Pine Lake Road, Suite 100
Lincoln, NE 68512
www.iuniverse.com
1-800-Authors (1-800-288-4677)

Cover by Myron Davis

ISBN-13: 978-0-595-35996-7 (pbk)
ISBN-13: 978-0-595-80447-4 (ebk)
ISBN-10: 0-595-35996-5 (pbk)
ISBN-10: 0-595-80447-0 (ebk)

Printed in the United States of America

In Memory of My Mother

Acknowledgments

I doubt if my story would've been published if it wasn't for two special ladies:

My cousin, Judy Farrell, for her help and guidance, but most of all, her patience. When most of my friends felt I was wasting my time, she encouraged me to continue.

Sherri Schutte, who never tired of editing my story, no matter how many times I changed it. I also want to thank her husband, Tad, and her three daughters, Caroline, Victoria, and Elizabeth for never complaining about the time she spent with me.

And, a special thanks goes to Myron Davis, the photographer who captured the perfect photo for the cover.

Chapter 1

▼

Twelve-year-old Carl Sanford woke to the smell of bacon and waffles. When his father was home, and not working far out in the Gulf, he always fixed breakfast. Carl looked forward to those treasured early mornings spent with his father, eating and talking. He seldom ate breakfast when his father worked; his mother never got up early and rarely missed an afternoon nap. She would be in bed when he left for school and when he returned.

Ever since summer, Carl had been eager for Christmas vacation to begin. Now, there were only seven days left before Christmas and he was anxious to spend the next five with his father aboard *Captain Jack*, his father's shrimp boat. It had been another year of unpleasant memories and the situation he struggled with had gotten worse; he hoped that being away from home would help. *Maybe this time I'll have the courage to tell Dad.*

When Carl and his father finished loading his father's truck, they returned to his mother's bedroom and kissed her good-bye. For Carl, it was more of an obligation than a show of love or respect; she had insisted he wake her and give her a kiss before going to school or leaving home. It was 1951, and not since the war had he been comfortable kissing his mother.

On the way from their home in Fort Myers to Fort Myers Beach, where *Captain Jack* was berthed, they picked up Butch, the man who worked for his father. Butch was a large, compassionate man with a sense of humor that kept Carl laughing. Carl looked forward to the five days he would be working beside him.

"I see we have a full crew today," Butch said while getting in the truck. "Good to see you again, Carl."

Carl thought how small his hand felt in Butch's large, calloused hand. "Good to see you, Butch." Butch had insisted Carl call him "Butch."

It was still dark that morning when Carl's father woke him, which added to the length of a day filled with hard work. Carl was tired and had turned in early. He fell asleep listening to the steady roar of *Captain Jack's* huge engine—its large muffler and exhaust pipe were located aft of the bulkhead next to his berth.

It seemed to Carl that he had not been sleeping long when static from the boat's radio and a familiar voice woke him. He lifted his head from his pillow and listened. The voice was coming from the radio. It was Tom, his father's brother:

"*Captain Bill* calling *Captain Jack*. Over."

"This is *Captain Jack*. Over."

"Hi, Doc." Carl had never heard anyone but Tom call his father "Doc." "I hate to tell you this, but what you suspect is happening—is. Over."

"Are you sure? Over."

"Yes.... It's your best friend. Over."

"Bob? Over."

"I'm afraid so. Over."

"That son-of-a-bitch!...Did he tell you? Over."

"No. I overheard him telling some of his friends. And from the way they were talking; he's not the only one. Over."

"I shoved off four hours ago. Do you think he's still there? Over."

"I wouldn't doubt it. Over."

"I'm turning around. I'll talk to you later. And thanks, Tom. Over."

"Be careful. Over."

"I will. Over and out."

From his berth, the upper berth, Carl watched his father change course then heard him call Butch. Butch slept on the lower berth.

"Butch, wake up!"

"I heard," Butch answered.

"I'm sorry, Butch. I know you and your family were counting on this trip to pay for Christmas. But don't worry, I'll make it up to you."

"Thanks. But it sounds like your problem is bigger than mine. Is there anything I can do?"

"Just stand by and take care of Carl. There may not be anything to this. If not, we'll top off our fuel and ice and be back out here in the morning."

Carl's thoughts were mixed. He wanted his father to find out how unfaithful his mother was, but did not want them to get a divorce. He was worried.

Not long after waking Butch, his father asked him to take the helm. While Butch steered, his father put on his foul-weather gear, then stepped out into the cold night. After an hour or so of pacing the deck, he returned. When Carl heard the cabin door open, he closed his eyes and pretended to be asleep. He felt it would be best if his father thought he was sleeping and had not heard him talking with Tom.

Even though Carl's berth was located in the back of the cabin, he could still see the helm and through the windshield. It had been a beautiful day, but soon after the sun set, storm clouds began to build, and the sky became dark and threatening. It was not long before the inside of the cabin was the same as the night—black. The only light was the compass light, which Butch kept turned off most of the time. Seldom did he turn it on, and then for only a second or two.

By the lightning ahead, Carl knew they were headed into a storm, and when rain began hitting the windshield, he heard his father say, "We sure as hell don't need this!"

"Looks like it's going to be a bad one. Don't you think we should stay out here and ride 'er out?" Butch had asked the question Carl wanted asked.

"Probably." Carl heard the disappointment in his father's voice. "Slow her down a little, but hold your course. Maybe it'll clear up by the time we get to San Carlos light. If not, we'll turn north, into the wind, and wait until morning." He paused a few minutes. "We have about two hours before we get to the light. You might as well get some sleep."

"I don't mind staying up and helping."

"Thanks, but I need to do some serious thinking."

"I understand."

Carl struggled with whether to stay in his berth or go to his father. He felt sorry for him, standing at the helm, alone, upset, and worried. He wanted to comfort him and be comforted, but felt certain that his father had rather him not know his mother was cheating. He would always wish he had gone to him, even if for no other reason than to be by his side.

The silhouette of his father standing at the helm when the lightning flashed, the rain against the windshield, and the steady purr of the big engine was etched in Carl's mind. A memory to return many times, especially, in storms.

The rain had slackened some when Carl heard his father say, "Well, look at that."

"What?" Butch asked from his berth.

"San Carlos light is dead ahead."

Carl smiled when he saw the blinking light through *Captain Jack's* bleary windshield. His father had navigated in a storm to within three miles of his destination.

Soon after *Captain Jack* reached the buoy at the entrance of San Carlos Bay, the storm intensified, and there was enough light from the bolts of lightning for Carl to see that Butch had joined his father at the helm. He watched the reflectors on the channel markers light up as Butch shined the searchlight while his father maneuvered from one marker to the next. The searchlight was mounted on top of the cabin; the handle that controlled it was located on the inside, above the helm, close to the ceiling.

"It's too early for the bridge tender to be there," Butch said. "So I guess we'll have to tie up at the docks north of the bridge."

"I sure as hell don't look forward to the long walk to my truck in this weather, but I don't have a choice."

"Why don't you just wait til morning?" Butch asked.

"I can't.... I have to go tonight.... Even if I have to swim ashore."

His father was silent for a moment. "Do you think you and Carl can dock and tie up *Captain Jack* without me?"

"No problem, especially with the wind blowing from the Northwest. What do you have in mind?"

"Since the tide is high, and it'll be calm in the bay, you could back *Captain Jack* up to the seawall that's close to my truck. Then I can jump off. What do you think?"

"I think it's a crazy idea. Putting the bow close to the seawall would be much easier, but it's too high to jump from. So, if you're sure that's what you really want to do, we'll give it a try."

Carl pretended to be asleep when his father gently shook him.

"Carl. Wake up."

"What's up?"

"I have to go ashore for a while, and I need you to help Butch tie up the boat. OK?"

"OK."

His father turned on the cockpit lights, which provided enough light in the cabin for Carl to see how to get around. The lightning had let up, but the rain had increased, which added to the black of an already gloomy night.

"Are you still awake?" his father asked.

"Yes, I'm awake."

"Butch is going to back close to the seawall, and when it's close enough, I'll jump off. I want you to stand in the companionway and watch me. Tell Butch as soon as you see me jump. That way he can put the boat in forward and it won't drift back into the seawall. So, remember, as soon as I jump, tell Butch."

"I will. But, Dad, it's too dark. You won't be able to see where you're going to land."

"Don't worry. I'll make it."

Since Carl didn't ask his father why he was leaving the boat, he would always feel that his father knew he was aware of his mother's cheating.

Carl stood by his father's side and watched while he used the searchlight to locate a place safe enough for Butch to back up to.

"That looks good," his father said to Butch.

Butch began backing to where his father was shining the light, and when *Captain Jack* got close to the seawall, Carl's father turned off the searchlight; he didn't want to be blinded by the light when he looked back at Carl to give him instructions.

Before Carl's father stepped out on the slippery deck, he bent down and kissed him on the cheek.

"I love you, Carl. I'll see you in the morning."

Saying "I love you" was something his father rarely did. He wondered if his father was worried about him having to deal with the trauma of a divorce.

Carl's eyes burned from the rain, but he didn't take them off his father as he cautiously made his way aft. The glow of his father's yellow foul-weather suit, lit by the cockpit lights and blurred by the rain, was a picture that would always be with him.

He couldn't see the seawall, but when his father put his hands up and motioned, in a cautious manner, to come back a little more, he shouted to Butch, "You're getting close!"

Butch continued to let the boat drift back toward the seawall. "Let me know when he looks like he's ready."

"I will!" Carl watched his father sit on the gunwale. "He's sitting on the gunwale!" When his father swung his legs over the gunwale, waved, and pushed himself off, Carl shouted, "He jumped!"

Butch shoved the throttle forward; the engine revved, and *Captain Jack* surged away from the seawall. With his head still out in the rain, Carl braced himself against the companionway opening and struggled to see his father. He could hear the water from *Captain Jack's* large propeller blasting against the seawall, but could not see his father. The rain was too heavy.

Carl and Butch had just finished a late breakfast and were cleaning the galley. They had hoped his father would be back in time to join them.

"Uh-oh," he heard Butch say.

He looked down the dock to see what Butch was looking at. His mother and Bob, the man who was supposed to be his father's best friend, were walking arm in arm toward the *Captain Jack*.

"I wonder what they're up to?"

"I don't know," Butch answered. "But I do know one thing…this ain't good."

By the time they arrived, Carl and Butch were off the boat and on the dock. His mother opened her arms and ran the last few steps. He saw that her eyes were red and filled with tears.

"What's wrong?" he asked.

She wrapped her arms around him, something she had not done in years. "Your dad is no longer with us."

"What do you mean, he's not with us?"

"His truck slid off the road, hit a tree, and caught fire."

Carl pushed her back to arms length. "Where is he now?"

"He didn't make it. He was too badly burned."

"He must've been speeding and skidded on the slippery road." Then, crying uncontrollably, he buried his face in his mother's chest.

"But, why was he driving to town at that time of night?" his mother asked.

Carl backed away from his mother and went to Butch. He watched Butch's face and eyes turn from grief to anger as he glared first at Bob and then his mother. With his face pressed against Butch's large chest, he heard him say, "You know why!"

Carl felt certain that his father would still be alive if he had exposed his mother's infidelity. Even though he was only twelve, he still felt responsible.

*　　*　　*　　*

Carl's life had been about the same as any other twelve-year-old boy's, but soon after his father's death, it made a drastic change: His mother sold the *Captain Jack*, traded her debt free car for one with payments, traded that one when he was fourteen for one with a larger payment, and traded again when he was sixteen for one with an even larger payment. She said he could use it if he made the payments. He had agreed.

It was difficult for Carl to watch his mother party almost every night and squander all the money from the sale of the boat and his father's life insurance, but that did not compare to the hurt he felt when she consumed too much alcohol. She never admitted to being an alcoholic, but it was obvious to everyone that she was.

The memory of seeing his mother intoxicated and the many embarrassing situations he had to endure would be with him for the rest of his life.

Chapter 2

▼

Carl had hoped the Fort Myers truck stop would not be crowded, but it was. He had an uneasy feeling that everyone was watching him and wondering what he was up to. It was not that he had not done this before, he had, which caused him to question why he felt so nervous and insecure. To avoid making eye contact, he fixed his eyes on the "Restrooms" sign in the far back corner.

When he noticed the man ahead of him was also headed for the door marked "Men," he stopped at the magazine rack and casually began thumbing through a boating magazine. He would have preferred to look at one of the many "girlie" magazines, but did not want to attract the attention of the customers. In 1955 the magazines at truck stops were always more risqué than the Arcade Book Store where he and his buddies went to drool and fantasize over the latest, scantily clad centerfolds.

When Carl saw the man leave the restroom, he looked around to see if another was waiting, there wasn't. He placed the magazine back on the rack. Then, while searching in his pocket for the two quarters he knew were there, he nonchalantly headed for the door.

For some reason, even though he had used the machine several times before, he found it difficult to get his money in the slot. When he did, and thinking that one may not be enough, he bought two. *This time is going to be different. I'm going to use one of these, or maybe both.* The condoms he purchased before had spent their life in his wallet.

With his purchase secure in his pocket, for easy access, he stopped at the counter and bought a package of gum. He almost never chewed gum, but didn't feel comfortable walking out without buying something. While walking toward his car, he glanced at the gum, wondered why he had felt the need to buy it, then tossed it on the passenger side of the seat.

As he eased away from the truck stop and back on US 41, he read the sign beside the road: Punta Gorda 23 Miles. It was not a new sign; he had read it many times, but this time it had more meaning. There were only 23 miles separating him from the girl that was to be his first. A girl he had never met.

A rush of exhilaration and a feeling of accomplishment flowed through him when he felt the power and heard the tires squeal as he pressed the accelerator of his pride and joy—his '47 "Chevy" coupe. It was just that morning when he finished fine-tuning the freshly overhauled engine.

He was not aware of the engine being in bad condition when he traded his Cushman "Eagle" motor scooter for the Chevy. But even if he had known, he would have still traded. His only regret was that he had spent many weeks bumping out dents, sanding, masking, and painting before he discovered that the engine was in need of a major overhaul.

Removing the engine and replacing it without scratching the new paint had been difficult, but he managed to do it without making a single scratch. Not only did his friends and teachers recognize his mechanical abilities, they admired his patience.

Three months before he acquired his Chevy, a man who owned a boat at the marina where he worked, mentioned that his son was looking for a motor scooter. The man asked him if he would be interested in trading his scooter for a '47 Ford he owned. Carl was familiar with the car and had admired it many times. It was in excellent condition.

He wondered why the man would ever consider parting with it, and was shocked even more when he realized the man didn't expect any additional money. It would be an even trade.

After accepting the man's offer, and trying to control his excitement, he rushed to tell his boss about his good fortune and ask if he could have some time off. His boss, who was also a close friend, was pleased that Carl had made such a fine trade and told him to take all the time he needed. Carl's heart felt as if it were going to beat right out of his chest as he hurried home to pick up his title and tell his mother. He found it difficult to keep his speed under control.

Her bedroom door, as usual, was closed; she was taking her afternoon nap. He cautiously knocked; no response; he knocked a little louder; still no response. *At least she's taking a nap and not entertaining one of her many man friends.*

Controlling his desire to share his news became too much; he opened the door. His nostrils filled with the familiar smell of rancid perspiration mixed with cheap perfume, aftershave, and whiskey—she drank almost any liquor, but preferred whiskey. Her room always smelled similar, but this time was worse. It was obvious that a man had left not long before he arrived.

"Haven't I told you to never come in my bedroom when I'm taking a nap!" she screamed.

"Yes. But I have some fabulous news."

"It better be!"

"I just traded my motor scooter for a '47 Ford coupe that's in mint condition."

"You mean you traded without asking my permission!" Her eyes opened wide and her lips tightened to about the size of a prune and just as wrinkled. She rose to a sitting position and glared at him while waiting for his answer.

He had seen that look many times before. And, like a blow to the stomach, it dawned on him that he had made a humongous mistake—he had made a decision without consulting her. What had been a glorious moment had quickly turned into one of his worst.

"I'm sorry," he said, expressing regret for not getting her permission. "I guess I should've asked, but I was just so excited…. This car is really clean, and all the owner wants is my motor scooter and no additional cash. An opportunity like this doesn't come around too often. It's a fantastic deal."

"I don't care how clean it is or how good the deal is, you can't have it! I'll buy you a car when you graduate, and you can't have one until then. And that's final! Now get out and get back to work!"

"Please, Mom," he pleaded, trying to be humble and not anger her more than he had by waking her. "A car would be much safer than my motor scooter and it's such a good deal." There had been many times when he had to hold back his temper, swallow his pride, and endure her thoughtless, harsh decisions. This time had affected him more than the others; he was disappointed and found it difficult to deal with his grief. He had not shed a tear since his father's death and funeral, but was close. "Please, Mom."

Her glare became more intense. "I told you I would buy you a car when you graduate!" she said through clenched teeth. "Now, get out!"

"Why do I have to wait?"

"Because I said so!"

Her answer destroyed his ability to be patient, and his anger increased to a point where he could no longer control his temper.

"You're going to buy me a car! You wouldn't have one now if it wasn't for me making the payments!"

"You can't talk to me in that tone of voice!" she shouted. "And I'll hear no more of it!"

"I've never thought it was fair of you to expect me to pay the payments then allow me to use it just one night a week. So…if I can't have a car, neither can you!"

"What do you mean by that smart remark!"

He looked her straight in the eyes. "I've made my last payment!"

"You'll make the payments or you won't use it!"

"There's one thing for sure: If I don't make the payments, you won't be driving it much longer, either."

"You better watch your smart mouth! And you better make the payments!"

"Can I trade for the car?"

"No! Definitely no!"

"Then I won't make another payment."

She swung her legs off the side of her bed, as if to stand. "If you know what's good for you…"

"Not another payment!" he shouted, then turned and hit the closed door with his fist, splitting one of the heavy panels.

When his mother stood and made a fist, he moved toward her. With his eyes glaring down at hers he saw how shocked she was to see that instead of stepping back, he had stepped closer. He knew she realized he was no longer going to take her blows. She had hit him her last time.

He continued to keep his eyes fixed on hers until she lowered her fist and shifted her eyes to the side. Without saying a word, he slowly turned his back to her and walked out of her room.

Before going back to work, he called his friend, Ralph, and asked if he wanted to trade his motor scooter for the Ford. Ralph was thrilled. He knew the car and was anxious to trade. Carl figured if someone other than he was going to be the beneficiary of a great deal, he wanted it to be his best friend.

Carl had lived next door to Ralph since they were nine years old. Each bought their Cushman "Eagles" at about the same time; both were in extremely bad condition. Carl and Ralph worked on them every night and weekend until they were the best looking and fastest in all of Lee County.

That afternoon, Carl introduced Ralph to the man who owned the Ford. Later, when he realized he should've defied his mother and traded, he regretted calling Ralph. The many years of strict discipline had caused him to react to his mother's command without giving it any thought.

The large smile, his boss greeted him with, soon vanished when they made eye contact. Carl saw that his boss understood, and was pleased that he didn't ask any questions.

It took two months of searching before Carl found his '47 Chevy. It took that long to find someone willing to trade their car for his scooter. The money from not making the two payments on his mother's car was all the money he had to get it looking and running like the car it was. Not only had his work on the Chevy been a major accomplishment, it reflected his mechanical ability, and encouraged his independence.

Before trading, he found it difficult to avoid his mother's criticism and demands, but once he began working on his car, he became totally involved and was able to ignore her screams and threats. She had always been demanding and self-centered, but had gotten much worse since his father's death. Defying her was something he was not comfortable with, but he had decided that four years of being patient with her abuse and domination was long enough.

It was his belief that his mother's decision to not let him buy the Ford was the reason he found the courage to defy her and start making decisions without asking her permission. In the past, he had shown her the respect a mother deserves and had never disobeyed her or—unlike the fights the neighbor kids had with their parents—raised his voice in anger.

Even though he knew his decision to ignore her was right, he felt uncomfortable when he did. And he wondered why. Especially after the many nights he had listened to the sounds of pleasure coming from her bedroom when his father was working far out in the Gulf.

A few days after Carl traded, which was more than two months after making the last payment on his mother's car, a man came to their door. "I'm here for the money or the car," the man said to his mother.

She glared at Carl. "I guess you're happy now!" she shouted. "You've caused me to lose my car!" Then turned back to the man. "Just take the damn thing!…Now that my son is a 'know-it-all' teenager, I'm better off without one."

To avoid the blinding lights of the oncoming cars, Carl found that he was driving too close to the edge of the road; he had even driven off a few times. Only once before had he driven at night on US 41, or "The Tamiami Trail" as most knew it by, especially those living between Tampa and Miami. It was an experience he would never forget.

He had accompanied his mother and one of her many man friends to Miami. He would have preferred to stay home, but his mother insisted he go. Looking back, he figured she already knew he would be the one driving when they returned. He was only fourteen.

Soon after arriving in Miami, his mother and her friend began drinking. Before leaving Miami, they stopped at one more bar. Carl waited in the car.

He was stretched out in the back seat and almost asleep when he saw them staggering toward him. The man was carrying a brown paper bag, which Carl knew contained a new bottle of cheap whiskey.

"You're always asking to drive, so drive us home," his mother slurred.

"I've never driven at night," he pleaded, "and I've only driven this car a few times. I don't think I can. And besides, I don't even have a driver's license."

"Well, hell," the man said, "if the kid don't wanna drive, I'll drive."

"That's OK," Carl said. "I'll drive." He had rather drive than be driven by the man who had frightened him many times while driving to Miami. And now that the man was intoxicated, he certainly didn't want to suffer with that experience.

Before Carl had even driven out of the bar's parking lot, the man leaned over the back of the front seat and pointed to the bottle of water on the front floorboard. "Hand me that jug of water. Your mother and I need a drink."

Carl was adjusting the rear-view mirror when he saw his mother turn up the bottle of whiskey, still in the bag, then the bottle of water. The man did the same.

He had barely left the city when he heard the man say something. He did not understand what the man said, and he could not see him in the mirror, so he turned his head to hear him better. Without asking what was said, he quickly turned his eyes back to the road. Seeing his mother lying on the seat with her shirt and bra off and the man leaning over her and fondling her breasts was an image that would never go away.

The trip from Miami to Fort Myers would be the most difficult 140 miles he would ever travel.

The challenges of driving his mother's big Buick for the first time at night were many: He had to learn when to dim his lights and when to blink them to encourage the others to dim theirs. Getting used to where the edge of the road was, while being blinded by the lights of those who chose not to dim theirs, was the most difficult. The pressure of learning to drive in those conditions was enormous, but, fortunately, the distractions were enough to keep him from thinking about what was happening in the back seat.

Even though it had been more than two years since that God-awful trip from Miami, it was on his mind and as clear as if it were the day before. He thought how he had struggled with that huge Buick, and admired how much easier his Chevy handled.

A large pothole brought his thoughts back to the present. Not only was the road to Punta Gorda narrow, it was in bad need of repair. He slowed a little and began concentrating on the bullbats darting in and out of his car's headlights, searching for insects. He marveled at how they could come so close to the car without getting hit.

I wonder if the bullbats dove at the lanterns on my grandfather's ox-drawn wagon when he made the trip to Punta Gorda?

Chapter 3

▼

A few days earlier, while Carl and Ralph were working on Carl's car, Ralph's older brother, Bobby, joined them.

"My girlfriend has a friend who wants to give you some," were Bobby's first words to Carl.

"What!"

"She wants to have sex with you."

"I know what you meant. But why?"

"I don't know why, but I'm pretty sure she does."

"What makes you think so?"

"The other night, while waiting for my girlfriend to get off work, her friend, one of the other waitresses, joined us at our table. During our conversation I asked if she was dating anyone. She said she wasn't and asked if I had someone in mind. So, knowing that Ralph has a girlfriend, I thought of you. When I told her about you, she seemed really interested."

Bobby worked for a restaurant supply company, and his girlfriend worked for one of his customers in Punta Gorda.

"What did you tell her?" Carl's curiosity was building.

"I told her you were sixteen, shy, and have never been laid."

"You didn't!"

"Yes, I did."

"What did she say?"

"She said, 'Tell him to come see me. I'll lay him.'"

"You're kidding me!"

"No, I'm not. My only regret is: I wish it was me."

"But, why would she say that, especially, when she hasn't even met me?"

"I don't know. But there's one thing for sure…she's no virgin. I think she's been with many, and it's my opinion that she enjoys being someone's first."

"Why do you think that?"

"Because, when I mentioned that you have never been with a woman, her expression brightened, and she seemed to become intrigued."

"I can't believe a girl I've never met, wants to have sex with me because I'm a virgin." He was beginning to get suspicious. "I have a feeling that you and this girl are playing a joke on me. I'm supposed to meet her, expecting to get laid, then, when I don't, you and she will laugh your asses off…. Right?"

"Have I ever played a joke on you?"

"No, you haven't. But, there's always a first time."

"I wouldn't do that. I'm sincere and I think she is too."

Knowing Bobby was not a practical joker, Carl believed him.

"When can I meet her?"

"She'll be working until ten o'clock every night this week. She said to come any night. She also said to be there around 9:30. That way, since there's hardly any customers after 9:30, she can sit with you."

This is too easy, something's not right. Either she's fat, or ugly, or both. Bobby hasn't said much about her looks, but he did say he wished he could be with her. That's encouraging…. "How old is she?"

"She looks about fifteen, but I think she has to be older than that to work at the restaurant."

"Her name is Eve," was Bobby's answer when Carl asked her name. He remembered thinking that "Eve" was not an appropriate name for the girl Bobby had described.

Since the restaurant was located right on US 41, Carl had no problem finding it. As he pulled into the almost empty parking lot, he began to notice just how nervous he was and how dry his mouth and throat were. While waiting for his courage to build, he spotted the gum; he thought chewing a piece would help his mouth and throat. And it did. When he was satisfied the gum had worked all its magic, he put it in the wrapper it came in, then dropped it in the ashtray.

It was exactly 9:30 when he opened the restaurant door. The only waitress he saw was busy cleaning and did not see him. There was not a sign saying "Hostess Will Seat You" so he picked a booth next to the window. He didn't want to look shy and sit in the back, nor did he want to look bold and sit up front. He wasn't comfortable sitting in a large booth alone, but was pleased with the location.

The waitress spotted him and began walking toward him; he hoped she was Eve; she was much better looking than he figured she would be.

"Hi. I'm Sally." Her voice was soft and her smile was large. "What can I get you?"

He was disappointed.... "I'll just have a Coke. I'm waiting for someone."

With her eyes fixed on his, Sally held her pencil to her pad without writing, then looked out the window. "Is that shiny, blue car yours?"

"Yes."

"And you're from Fort Myers?"

"Yes, again."

She paused for a moment, smiled and said, "You must be Carl!"

"How did you know?"

"Bobby and I are friends. He said you might be coming up this week. He said: 'look for a good-looking fellow driving a fabulous-looking blue car.' He was right with both descriptions."

"Thanks." He smiled, but before he could ask if Eve was working, she turned and rushed to the back. He watched as she disappeared into what he figured was the kitchen, pushing both swinging doors at the same time. Even before the doors stopped swinging, she reappeared with a much smaller waitress. The other waitress was there for only a few seconds before darting back into the kitchen.

Sally returned with his drink, placed it on the table in front of him, then sat in the seat opposite his. "So, you're Carl."

"Yep. I'm Carl." Her smile and evaluating eyes caused him to feel she knew why he was there. He became uncomfortable and almost wished he hadn't come. Then he looked up, and walking toward him was the waitress he saw earlier with Sally. She was one of the most beautiful girls he had ever seen. Her long blonde hair and shapely, well-proportioned, petite body was first to capture his attention. As she moved closer, he noticed that her deep, blue eyes were locked onto his.

"Is this Eve?" he asked.

Sally turned to see who he was looking at. "That's Eve. She would've been here sooner, but after seeing you, she had to go to the ladies room and freshen up a bit."

Carl stood at the same time Eve arrived at his table.

She offered her hand. "Hi. I'm Eve."

He took her hand in both of his; he found that he was staring without commenting. Her beautiful smile, her perfect lips, and her soft, sexy voice had distracted him. He cleared his throat, as if that was the reason. "Hi. I'm Carl."

Sally stood. "I have some more cleaning to do, so I better get to it. It was nice meeting you, Carl. And from the way you guys are looking at each other, I'm sure I'll see you again."

Eve slid into the seat Sally left and Carl returned to the seat across from her.

"You're not what I expected." He regretted what he said as soon as the words left his mouth.

"What did you expect?"

He was in a predicament. He couldn't say he was expecting someone who looked sleazy, sleazy enough to where her intentions were unmistakable. He wanted to tell her that she looked too innocent to offer to have sex with someone she had never met. He was starting to doubt what Bobby had told him. But, if she did offer to do what Bobby said, he didn't want to blow his opportunity by being naive and saying something that would discourage her.

"I guess I thought you'd be older, heavier, and a helluva lot less attractive."

Even though her smile reflected her pleasure with his compliment, she, teasingly, reached across the table and touched his hand. "You're just saying that."

"I'm saying it because it's true."

"Before it gets too late," she said, while returning her hand to her side of the table, "I need to let my mother know if I want her to pick me up. Can you take me home after work?"

"Uh, yeah.... Sure."

"I'll give her a call.... I'll be right back."

What was I thinking? he thought while admiring the movement of her petite behind as she walked to the phone. *I actually thought I was going to pick her up after work, drive to some lonely spot, take off our clothes, and have sex. Stupid! Stupid! Stupid! How could I have been so gullible?—But after what Bobby said, what else could I have thought.—I wonder if he was kidding and told me what he did just to get me to meet her?—Bobby wouldn't do that.—Maybe she was teasing, and he misread her.—I'm afraid I got my hopes up for nothing.—It's my own damn fault. I should've known better.*

"Well, that's taken care of," Eve said. "How long have you known Bobby?"

"Since I was nine."

"Bobby said you are sixteen."

"Yep. Sixteen."

"You look much older. Maybe it's your height. How tall are you?"

"Five-eleven."

"Where did you get that nice tan? Are you in the sun much? I bet you are; your hair looks as if it's bleached by the sun."

"I work at a marina."

"Do you lift weights or something?"

"No."

"Then how did you get those large muscles and broad shoulders?"

"I take after my dad."

"Do you look like your dad?"

"Yes."

"Are you and your dad close?"

"We were."

"Were?"

"He died when I was twelve."

She paused, her eyes drifted from his to the table. After a moment she reached across the table and took his hands in hers. "Carl," she said, while raising her eyes to his. "I'm trying really hard to have a conversation, but it seems to me that you are uncomfortable with me…. Are you?"

"No. Not really."

"I think you are…. Can we be open and honest with each other?"

"Sure. I'd like that."

"Did Bobby tell you that having sex with me is a sure thing?"

"I got that impression."

"Oh, Carl. I'm so sorry. When he described you, and even though I'm three years older than you, I wanted to meet you. Did he tell you that he told me you had never been with a girl?"

"Yes."

"And I crudely, blurted out that I would lay you?"

He looked down at his hands. "Yes, he did."

"I don't know why I said what I did. I was only kidding and didn't mean it. I thought he knew."

"You're nineteen?" With the many other comments he could've made, he chose to make that one.

"Yes. Most people think I look younger, but I don't mind. My youthful looks will be beneficial when I'm older."

Carl raised his eyes from their hands, and when his eyes met hers, they squeezed each other's hands. The disappointment Carl had felt had changed to comfort. Without taking his eyes from hers, he said, "I'm glad I came."

"You aren't disappointed?"

"I would be if you looked and acted like the girl I had imagined."

"I'm glad you came too…. But, I need to continue being honest…. A day after my talk with Bobby, I met a really nice guy. He's quite a bit older than me, and, except for him being nice, I don't know why I agreed to go out with him. We haven't gone out yet, but we made a date for this weekend. We may have only one. Who knows?"

"I understand." Carl could barely hear his own voice. "You probably wouldn't want to go with someone my age and still in school."

"Not true. If I hadn't made the date, and I didn't feel committed to keep it, I would love to go out with you. But I'm not sure you want to date me."

"Yes I do. And I regret that you made the date."

Carl saw that her eyes were sincere and expressed regret. A rush of desire surged through him as he watched her voluptuous lips form the words, "Me, too."

Again, they squeezed the other's hands.

"It's ten o'clock. We can go now," she said, then gently pulled her hands from his.

"Wow! I love your car!"

"Thanks."

"Bobby said you and his brother did a lot of work on it, but I had no idea it was this nice."

She surprised him by going to the driver's door. He opened it; she got in and slid to the other side.

"It took Ralph, that's Bobby's brother, and me several weeks of hard work before we were satisfied with its looks. We even overhauled the engine.... Which way?"

"South.... Have you named her?"

"Not yet. But I will. I name everything I own."

"Me, too." She turned toward him, smiled, and said, "Let's name her."

"All right. What name do you have in mind?"

"Let's see.... You chose a beautiful blue paint.... How about "Blue?""

"Blue.... My car, *Blue*. I like it. From now on, she's *Blue*. Yes. I like it a lot. Thanks."

She eased closer, kissed him on the cheek and said "I like you."

"I like you too," he said without taking his eyes off the road.

She pointed to the right. "Turn here!"

It was a small two-rut road. "You don't live on this road, do you?"

She moved even closer, "No. I live a little farther down the Trail," meaning the Tamiami Trail. "I want to talk some more. Anyhow, I'm not anxious to get home. Are you?"

"No.... Not at all." His mouth was getting dry again, and he was concerned about his breath. "I have some gum somewhere on the seat. Would you like a piece?"

"I'm sitting on it, and yes I would." She searched beneath her, found it, took two pieces out, removed the paper from both, then put one in his mouth.

Carl folded the warm gum with his tongue. The flavor seemed different, but special. It was as if it had been enhanced by her touch and the heat from her body. He caressed it and savored it until its warmth was no longer.

Carl was deep in the woods when the road came to a large cleared area and ended. Before turning the engine off, he turned *Blue* around. Fortunately, it was October, no mosquitoes, and warm enough to leave the windows open.

To face him, Eve positioned her left leg under her and twisted toward him.

"Something is really bothering me," she said.

"Oh?...What?"

"I wish, so much, that I hadn't acted like someone I'm not, and I don't want you, or Bobby, to have the wrong impression of me. I'm not going to tell you that I've never been with someone. I have. I've been with two. And I won't tell you that I didn't enjoy being with them. I did. I went with each for about six months. I stopped dating the last fellow six months ago, and I haven't been with anyone since."

Carl was stunned. "With your looks, and you said you enjoyed it, why has it been that long?" He watched her remove her gum and throw it out the window. He did the same.

She moved closer. "Because, until now, I haven't met someone I wanted."

The tips of her teeth glistened in the soft light of the moon as her lips parted and moved closer to his. Their first kiss was awkward. It took him a moment to get comfortable with how she preferred to kiss. She was leading, and he was eager to follow.

By their second kiss their lips fit perfectly; by the third, her tongue found his and his lips caressed it as it eased deeper and deeper.

There were several more passionate kisses before he found the courage to attempt to touch her breasts. He cautiously eased his hand up from her waist. This was not the first time he had made an effort to feel a girl's breasts, but it was his first without resistance. She wasn't wearing a bra.

He felt her hand unbuttoning his shirt, hinting she wanted it off. When they finished unbuttoning his shirt, she turned her back to him and he unzipped her dress. Before he could get his shoes, socks, pants, and shirt off, she was completely nude and helping him.

They came together and kissed while his hands touched and explored places he had only dreamed of. Their kisses became more intense with passion as he became comfortable with how she preferred to be kissed, and where. He felt her firm little body being pressed against his, and he knew he had to be dreaming when she pulled her lips from his and said, "Let's get in the back."

When he opened his door, the interior light came on; he found it difficult to believe her beauty. She was barely out when she wrapped her arms around his waist and, with her face against his chest, pressed her warm, naked body against his. With his cheek caressing her soft hair and his left arm around her upper back, he slowly moved his right hand down her smooth skin toward her waist, and beyond.

She raised her parted lips to his. Their kiss expressed their desire. And the cold, damp grass on their bare feet did little to dampen their passion. They continued to embrace as he reached for the back of the front seat and shoved it forward. She got in first.

He closed the door behind him, which left only the light from the full moon, enough light to see her outstretched, beckoning arms.

Her arms were tight around him, and their lips never separated as they became comfortable with the seat and each other.

"Damn!" he said. "My protection's in the pocket of my pants."

"That's OK," she whispered. She wrapped her arms around him and held him close. "I'm sure it's a safe time."

Chapter 4

When Carl drove away from Eve's home, and turned south toward Fort Myers, he found that he wasn't in a hurry. It was late, but he wasn't anxious to get home.

"What an experience!" he said out loud. "This will be a night we won't soon forget. Right, *Blue*?"

It was difficult for him to comprehend what had happened; his head was filled with questions: *What caused her to change her mind?—Did she think she deceived me by misleading Bobby and felt guilty? Then felt sorry for me and wanted to make it up to me? Or, did she know all the time what she was going to do?—Did she tell Bobby the truth, but was misleading me?—Was she not being honest with me when she said it had been more than six months?—She seemed so sincere when she asked me to come back next week. But, her date is this weekend, and this is Wednesday.—I think I'll return tomorrow.*

The feeling of anticipation, which had Carl's insides trembling, suddenly changed to anguish when he pulled in his driveway. Frank's car was there. Frank was the man his mother was dating. He didn't like Frank. Not even a little.

He was disappointed when, at one o'clock in the morning, he saw that most of the lights were still on. *They're awake and, most likely, intoxicated.* He wished there was a way to get to his bedroom without being seen.

The thought of listening to his mother's slurred words and sarcastic comments had him dreading to go in. But tolerating Frank's remarks would be even worse. More often than not, Frank added his "belittling" comments to whatever his mother said, which caused him to dislike Frank even more. It had been difficult when his mother and Frank teamed up to discipline him, but, by ignoring them, he had managed to avoid any major arguments. He hoped his luck would hold.

Frank met him at the door. "We have a problem!"

"What's our problem?" Carl asked.

"Your mother's in jail."

"Mom's in jail! Why?"

"She wrote a bad check."

"But why is she in jail? She's written bad checks before without being put in jail."

"She probably pissed off the man who owns the store where she cashed the check. When he came to collect his money, your mother was intoxicated, and instead of trying to work something out, she offered him a drink. He said he wanted his money, not a drink. She said she didn't have it and he'd just have to wait until she got some. Being that he had always been patient with her, she didn't believe him when he said he was going to see the sheriff.... Boy! Was she shocked when she saw the deputy pull in the driveway."

"Did the deputy say how much it'll take to get her out?"

"The check was for $100.00 and the fine is $50.00."

Carl wondered why Frank hadn't already gotten her out. "Are you going to get her out?"

"Hell, no! She got herself in this mess. Besides, she said you'd get her out."

"Me! I don't have that much money."

"I don't either. So, it looks to me like you have a problem."

"Thanks a lot."

Carl checked his wallet; he knew what was there, a twenty-dollar bill, but still checked. He held his wallet open for Frank to see. "Where can I come up with $130.00?"

"That's not my problem."

"Can't you help a little?"

"Nope."

Carl closed his wallet, then looked at Frank in disbelief as he shoved it in the back pocket of his Levi's. He came close to telling Frank what a jerk he thought he was, but realized it would be a waste of time. While shaking his head in disgust, he turned to leave.

"Hey! Where're you going? And what are you going to do about your mother?"

Still shaking his head and without answering, Carl continued toward his bedroom.

"Hello, Ralph." It was 6:00 A.M. Carl wanted to catch Ralph before he left for school.

"Good morning, Carl. I bet you're calling to tell me what a great time you had with Eve. Right?"

"I wish I were. Eve is a wonderful girl, but we'll talk about her later.... I have a problem and I need your help."

"Nothing happened to your car, did it?"

"No. *Blue's* fine."

"*Blue?*"

"That's what Eve named her."

"I'm anxious to hear about Eve.... What's your problem?"

"Mom's in jail."

"Somehow, that doesn't surprise me." Being Carl's best friend and neighbor, had exposed him to many instances of her selfish actions and fits of anger. One night he even helped Carl get her in the house after one of her many men had dumped her, drunk and half dressed, in her front yard.

"I'm not surprised either. And if I thought leaving her there for a few days would help, I would, but it won't. So, I have to get her out."

"I understand. How can I help?"

"I have to come up with $150.00. My boss has always liked my rifle, and here lately, he's been trying to get me to sell it to him. He said he'd give me fifty, and I have twenty, so that makes seventy. Do you have eighty bucks I can borrow for two weeks? That's about how much I'll make in two weeks."

"I only have forty, but Bobby's here. I'll ask if he has an extra forty.... He does, and you're welcome to it. He also asked how your date went. I told him you'd tell him later."

"Thanks.... And thanks for the money. I'll be over in a few minutes."

After a quick shower, he put his rifle in *Blue*, then walked next door to Ralph's. He figured Frank had stayed overnight when he saw his car still parked in the yard. Frank never used the driveway, even though it was wide enough for two cars.

Carl's boss was surprised to see him. "No school today?"

"Yes, there's school. I just dropped by to see if you're still interested in buying my rifle."

"Sure! I'd love to buy it. Fifty OK with you?"

"Fifty's fine. It's in my car. I'll get it."

When Carl returned with his rifle, his boss handed him a fifty-dollar bill.

"I sense that you have a problem. I'm not going to ask any questions, but, if there comes a time when you want your gun, you can buy it back for the fifty I'm paying."

"I appreciate your offer, but I really want you to own it."

"Will you be working this afternoon?"

"I'll be here.... I better hurry. I don't want to be late for school."

Instead of saying "take it easy," as Carl's boss always did, he said, "Good-luck."

Frank was sitting at the kitchen table with a cup of coffee when Carl arrived. "Did you come up with the money?"

"Yes," Carl said, while reaching for his wallet. "I'm almost late for school, so can you get her out?"

"Give me the money. I'll get your mother out for you." He made it sound like he was doing Carl a big favor.

Carl almost asked to be excused from his first class when he thought about the mistake he had made by giving Frank the money. He wondered if Frank would be intoxicated and his mother still in jail when he got home from school. It was a long day.

"You're home!" Carl said. He had prepared himself for the worst and was surprised when he saw his mother sitting on the couch with Frank.

"Hell yes I'm home! No thanks to you!" She patted Frank on the leg. "If it hadn't been for Frank, I'd still be there."

Carl looked at Frank, expecting him to explain, but all he got was a silly grin. It was clear that Frank had taken all the credit, and nothing he said would change how she felt. Saying anything would only make her think he was lying and trying to cause trouble. He looked at Frank until the grin disappeared and his eyes shifted to his hands. Then, and without commenting, he left for work.

On the way to work, Carl struggled with why he had not defended himself by exposing Frank for being the liar he was. It took only a few minutes of worrying about what he should have done before he wished he had left her in jail.

He was almost to work when it dawned on him that *Blue* was low on gas, and with no money for more, he would not be able, as he had planned, to drive back to Punta Gorda that night to see Eve. His anger increased when he realized it would be more than two weeks before he could see her again. Half of the paycheck he received the next day, Friday, would go to Ralph, the other half to Bobby, which left nothing for gasoline. The same for the following paycheck. There wasn't even enough gas to drive to school. He had to ride with Ralph.

Punta Gorda was a long distance call, but that wasn't the reason he did not call; he was ashamed for Eve to know he didn't have money for gasoline. He asked Bobby to tell her he would be back to see her as soon as he could.

It was Friday, the day Carl planned to drive to Punta Gorda. It had been sixteen days since he last saw Eve—a long sixteen days. The thought of being with her was always on his mind, which made it difficult to concentrate on work or school. His whole body ached each time he pictured them making love, and there had been many pictures.

"It won't be long now!" he said for only the bowl of Dinty Moore Beef Stew he was eating to hear. He had gassed up *Blue* as soon as he cashed his paycheck, and by not having to be at the restaurant until 9:30, he had plenty of time to eat, shower, and take a short nap. He wanted to be well rested.

While washing his dinner dishes, he looked out the window and saw his mother and Frank pull in the driveway. He tried to hurry and avoid them but was not fast enough.

"Hi, Son!"

He became uncomfortable when he noticed her exaggerated smile.

"Hi, Mom.... Frank."

"How about congratulating us."

He looked at her suspiciously. "For what?"

"For getting married!...We just got married."

"Congratulations," he forced out, but didn't offer to shake Frank's hand. He pretended his hands were still wet from washing the dishes.

After a few minutes of being polite, but avoiding their desire to involve him in their conversation, he noticed that his mother's eyes were getting that familiar, wild look, and her mouth was beginning to tighten and wrinkle. He knew he was going to be disciplined, insulted, or humiliated.

She continued to glare at him. "Now that there's a man in the house, things are going to be a lot different." She paused, then looked at Frank. "Now's as good of time as any for you to do what you said you were going to do." She looked back at Carl. "Frank wants to have a private talk with you."

"Let's go outside," Frank said.

It was obvious, by the anger, mixed with pleasure he saw in his mother's eyes, that she and Frank were up to no good. He watched his mother's lips form a devious smile as he slowly dried his hands. Before joining Frank, he held the door open for a moment, looked back at her, and wondered why she was so anxious for Frank to talk with him.

"What do you want to talk about?"

Without saying a word, Frank spun around and slapped him with all his might.

Carl put his hand to his stinging face and ringing ear, then, with his eyes fixed on Frank's, he lowered his hand and moved his face to within a few inches of Frank's. "Before I beat you until you can't talk.... I'd like to know what that was for!"

"There can only be one man of the house, and I'm it. Maybe now you'll remember that."

Carl took a step back. "I've already forgotten. You may have to remind me."

Frank made the mistake of swinging at Carl again, this time with his fist, not his open hand. Carl blocked Frank's punch with his left arm then hit him with his right fist, busting his left cheek and eye. Frank fell to the ground, but, determined to teach Carl a lesson, he made another mistake; he stood and charged him. This time, Carl hit him with his left, busting the other cheek and eye. Even though Frank couldn't see him, he charged again. Carl stepped to the side and hit him in the stomach.

Carl could not help but feel sorry for Frank as he watched him crumple to his knees, then slowly fall on his side and curl into a fetal position. By the sound of Frank's moans, he knew he had really hurt him. But instead of helping him up, he chose to go in and confront his mother.

"I can't believe what your stupid husband did! I just bet you encouraged him, didn't you!"

His mother's eyes were dancing with anger. "He told me he was going to teach you a lesson and show you who's in charge. Since you think you're too big for me to discipline, and you refuse to listen to anything I have to say, I agreed that you needed to be taught a lesson." She smiled when she noticed the left side of his face was red and his eye was watery and starting to swell. "It looks like he did what he said he was going to do. Maybe now you'll show me more respect."

"If anything, I have less respect for you, and none for Frank.... You better go help him."

"What have you done!" she shouted back to Carl when she saw Frank.

With the bathroom door closed and locked, Carl wet a washcloth with cold water then held it to his face and eye. "I guess I won't be going to Punta Gorda," he said when he saw how much his face and eye had swollen. "Maybe tomorrow night?"

Carl was lying on his bed with a washcloth over his face when he heard his mother talking on the phone to his uncle. He could hear every word she said: "You have to do something with Carl. He has no respect for me and won't do anything I say. I got married today, and what did he do? He beat the hell out of my husband.... I don't know why. Who knows what's in the mind of a teenager? I only know he's out of control. I've tried to be patient with him, but the last few months have been unbelievable. He won't help around the house; he even caused me to lose my car. All he does is work on that piece of junk he calls a car. I don't know how much more I can stand.... Tonight? You're coming tonight?...Tonight is fine. You can see what he did to Frank, my husband.... Thanks, Tom. I'll see you in about an hour."

Tom lived in Naples, about forty miles south of Fort Myers. It had been more than a year since Carl last saw him. He and his uncle had always been close; especially after his father's death, but after hearing what his mother told him on the phone, he was concerned that his uncle might believe her.

He wondered what Tom would say when he arrived, and he wondered if his mother would be even more intoxicated. He hoped she would.

The image of Frank charging him then falling to the ground when he hit him was like a movie, in slow motion, playing over and over. The fight reminded him of when he was seven years old, and after getting beat by the neighborhood bully, his father taught him how to box. After a few days of training, he fought the much larger bully again. He could still feel how he strutted back to his house without looking back at the bully. He had waited until he reached the porch before turning to see him running home, crying. Carl's father never said he saw the fight, but Carl figured he had.

His thoughts shifted to Eve, and how not seeing her, as planned, was going to be difficult. He was tempted to get in *Blue* and drive to Punta

Gorda and wait in the restaurant's parking lot until she got off work. He pictured her small hands soothing his tingling face and her soft lips kissing his hurting eye, his burning cheek, and his craving lips. He was imagining how her lips would feel when he heard his mother let Tom in.

After greeting each other, he heard his uncle say, "What in the hell happened to you?" He had seen Frank.

"That's what Carl did to him," his mother answered. "Frank.... I'd like you to meet Tom, Carl's uncle.... Soon after we got home from getting married, Carl asked Frank outside and did this."

"What in God's name caused him to do that?"

"I don't know why he does any of the things he does. He won't listen to me and, evidently, he hates Frank."

It pleased Carl to hear his uncle say, "I can't believe Carl would do this without being provoked.... Where is he?"

Carl was leaving his room when his mother said, "He's in his bedroom."

"Hi, Carl."

"Hi, Tom." Carl had never referred to his uncle, as uncle, and definitely not "Uncle Tom."

"What happened to your face and eye?"

"Mom is right about one thing, I don't like Frank, and I like him even less, now that the SOB took me out back and slapped me."

"Why did he do that?" Tom asked.

"He said he wanted to show me who the man of the house was."

"That's a damn lie!" his mother shouted, then moved her face a few inches from his. "Why do you want to lie? You know that's not what happened!"

Tom got between them. "Step back, Lois, before the fumes from your breath make the boy drunk." He shoved her away from Carl..."Now, after he slapped you, what happened?"

"I thought he was smart enough not to slap me again, but I was wrong. This time, I blocked his punch, and hit him. And to keep him from hitting me again, I had to hit him two more times."

"Are you going to believe a damn teenager!" his mother shouted.

"Yes, Lois, I am." He glanced at Frank lying on the couch. "And I'm sure glad Carl took care of the situation. If he hadn't…I would've." Then, while glaring at her, but pointing to Frank, he said, "And if I had…that son of a bitch would be in a lot worse condition."

"I don't know why I called you. You haven't liked me from the first day I married your brother!"

"You're wrong. I have never liked you."

"It's obvious that Carl can't live with us. So, since you think I'm not fit to raise him, I suggest you take him back with you. Maybe then you'll understand how difficult he is to deal with."

"That's a good idea. At least he won't be exposed to your drinking and vulgar lifestyle, or," he pointed to Frank, "have to tolerate that asshole on the couch." He looked toward Carl, "What do you think? Do you want to move to Naples and live with me and my family?…We'd love to have you."

"I'm sure I'd be happier living with you, but I'd hate to change schools. I only have one more year before I graduate. And I'd have to give up my job."

"Jill, my new wife's daughter, is your age and in the eleventh grade. So it wouldn't be like you won't know anyone in school. She's only been going to Naples High for two months. That's when her mother and I married and she moved to Naples. She says it's the best school she's ever attended. She loves it.

"And, in regard to losing your job, I need someone to clean my boat when I get in from a charter. I'll pay you to clean my boat each day after school. I'll also pay you to go out with me on weekends, help those who charter my boat catch fish, clean the fish they catch, and wash the boat when we return. With tips and what I pay you, I'm sure you'll make more than you make now. What do you think?"

"You make it sound wonderful."

"Living with us will be a helluva lot better than living in this crap. I know it'll be difficult to change schools and leave your friends…"

"Except for Ralph, I don't have any friends…. Are you sure I won't be a problem for you and your new family?"

Tom put his arm around Carl and patted him on the shoulder. "Don't worry about being a problem. You'll be comfortable living with us, and we'll be comfortable having you."

At that moment, moving to Naples and changing schools didn't bother him near as much as being an additional forty miles from Eve.

"I'd like to think about it through the weekend."

Tom tightened his hand on Carl's shoulder. "I understand."

"I'll call you on Sunday and let you know what I decide. If I decide to move in with you, I'll have to let my boss know, pack my clothes, and load my car. Then on Monday morning I'll check out of school, drive to Naples, and enroll in my new school."

Tom glanced at Carl's mother, then Frank, and back to Carl. "Do you think it's wise to stay another day with your mother and," he looked toward Frank, "this idiot?"

"What's he going to do…beat me up?"

Tom laughed. "I don't think he has the balls to try that again." Tom opened his arms to Carl, and as they hugged, he said, "I'm really looking forward to you living with us."

Tom motioned with his head to Carl, and without saying another word to Carl's mother, they walked outside.

"I'll call," Carl said when Tom waved from his truck.

Carl saw that Ralph was home, so instead of going back in and listening to his mother tell him what she thought of his uncle, he walked next door to talk with Ralph. He and Ralph had always shared their problems, and he was anxious to get Ralph's opinion of his latest crisis.

Ralph met him at the door. "Bobby and I saw your fight with that man. Boy, did you do a number on him! Who is that character?"

"He's Mom's new husband."

"Your mom's new husband! Why did he pick a fight with you?"

"That was his way of convincing me that he was in charge; the 'man-of-the-house;' the new 'top dog.'"

"What an imbecile," Bobby said as he joined them. "I'll bet he was surprised."

"When we didn't see you come out after an hour or so, we were going to come over," Ralph said, "but we saw you had company."

"That was my uncle. He wants me to live with him in Naples."

"Are you?" Ralph asked.

"I'm not sure. I told him I'd let him know this Sunday."

"Are you still driving to Punta Gorda tonight?" Ralph knew Carl had planned to see Eve that night.

"Not tonight. Maybe tomorrow night."

"Oh, by the way," Bobby said. "Eve asked me to let you know that she and her new boyfriend are getting along just fine. I think they're engaged."

"Engaged! She's only been going with him a little more than two weeks."

"I know. Maybe he has money."

"Eve wouldn't marry for money."

"Hell, Carl, she's only a whore. What makes you think she wouldn't marry for money?"

"She's not a whore!" he said through clenched teeth while glaring at Bobby. When Bobby lowered his eyes, and without saying another word, Carl turned and headed for home. He sensed that Bobby had no idea how strong his feelings were for Eve.

By the time he was home, he had decided that instead of waiting until Sunday to call his uncle, he would call the next morning. He had made up his mind.

Chapter 5

The size of Fort Myers, in 1955, was small enough for most everyone to know that Carl's mother was an alcoholic and also aware of her sleazy lifestyle. So, the next day when Carl mentioned to his boss that he was moving to Naples, and Sunday would be his last day, his boss wished him luck without asking any questions.

By Monday morning, Carl was packed and ready to begin his new adventure. School was his first stop, then on to Naples. When he arrived in Naples, and before going to his uncle's house, he stopped at Naples High and enrolled. He had gotten all the information he needed for enrolling when he talked to his uncle on the phone. He would start attending school the next day.

Carl thought back to the last time he was in Naples; he was eleven years old and with his father. His father was there to paint the name, WHY KNOT, on the transom of a new boat built by Guy Daniels Boat Works. Guy and his father had been close friends.

Carl remembered how shocked he was when on the way home, his father asked, "How would you like to learn to drive?"

"I'd love to!"

"I know the perfect place."

"Where?"

"Vanderbilt Beach."

"Have they built a road and bridge to it?"

"No. But my uncle has a barge on the mainland that we can drive the truck on and pole across to the beach."

The road from US 41 to the barge was a sandy, two-rut road, but his dad's Model-A Ford truck made it with little effort. After poling to the back side of the beach and driving off the barge, they had, for as far as they could see and in both directions, a whole beach to themselves. His father laughed at his mistakes, and praised his accomplishments, and it was not long, thanks to his father's patience, before he was comfortable driving. His father bragged on him all the way home. It was a day filled with pride and joy.

Before going to his uncle's house, Carl drove around and checked out the city; it was smaller than he remembered. He found it odd that among the few stores and businesses, there was only one bank, one hardware store, and one grocery store, but two bars and two liquor stores.

When Carl saw the Guy Daniels Boat Works sign, and without giving it any thought, he pulled into the parking area. He was not sure if he was allowed in the area where the boats were built and repaired, so he walked around the outside of the buildings. When he turned the corner of the last building next to the dock, he came to an abrupt stop. *WHY KNOT* was tied to the dock.

It had been more than five years since he watched, and occasionally helped, his father paint that name, but five years was not long enough to keep the tears of pride from filling his eyes. He stared at the name for a few moments, then, before someone saw him, he walked back to *Blue*.

Joyce, his uncle's wife, who he had never met, seemed pleased that he had chosen to stay with them and exerted much effort into making him feel welcome and comfortable.

"I can hardly wait for Jill, that's my daughter, to meet you." Joyce said, while helping Carl unpack. "Tom told her you were a little, fat kid.... Boy! Is she going to be surprised!"

Carl felt his face blushing. He turned away from Joyce and acted as if he was organizing his clothes in the closet.

"Tom told me she is also sixteen and a Junior."

"Yes she is. Her birthday was in September. The same month Tom and I were married. What month is yours?"

"July.... Did you get married on her birthday?"

"Yes, we did. It's what Jill wanted.... Tom was the first man I dated, after her father's death, who showed her any respect. Most had no desire to include her in our activities. But your uncle was different. He never wanted to leave Jill behind; she was involved in everything we did. And most of the time, if she wanted us to be, we were included in her activities. The patience and admiration Tom showed Jill, and the love and respect she expressed for him, is one of the many reasons I fell in love with him."

"Tom is a very caring guy. He reminds me of my dad.... Jill sounds like a really neat girl.... I'm looking forward to meeting her."

"I doubt if you'll like her. She's short and dumpy, has long straggly hair, is spoiled rotten, and extremely selfish.... Please be patient with her."

"I will if what you say is true, but, by the smile you're trying to hide, I think you're exaggerating."

"You'll see. She should be home in a few minutes.... Make yourself comfortable. And give me a call if you need anything. I'll be in the kitchen."

Carl was still getting accustomed to his room when he heard Joyce say, "Carl." He turned to see what she wanted. She and a very attractive girl, who he assumed was Jill, entered his room. It seemed to him, by Joyce's smile, that she enjoyed seeing how startled they were.

"Carl, this is my daughter, Jill.... Jill, this is Carl."

"Hi," they said.

He slowly removed his eyes from Jill's and looked at Joyce—she was still smiling. "I knew you were exaggerating.... Short and dumpy."

"Mommm! Is that what you told him?"

"I wanted him to expect the worst. Just like Tom prepared you for a short, fat, little fellow."

Jill's eyes drifted from his feet to his head. "Well, he's not short, and he definitely isn't fat."

"And you certainly aren't short and dumpy, nor is your hair long and straggly. And I doubt if you are spoiled rotten or selfish."

"I'm not. And I'm pleased to see that you're not what Tom had described. What else did Mom tell you?"

"That's all. But I had an idea she was kidding. I couldn't imagine a mother as attractive as yours having an unattractive daughter."

"That was a nice compliment," Joyce said. "If it were only true."

"It's true."

"I'll leave you two to get acquainted," Joyce said. "I'm going to finish dinner."

Carl couldn't think of anything to say; he was still trying to get over the shock of Jill's stunning beauty. Her glistening, straight black hair was cut short, and her casual, loose-fitting shirt and tight-fitting jeans concealed little of her shapely body. He couldn't tell if she was wearing makeup, but if she was, it was just enough to highlight her black, almond-shaped eyes and her perfectly shaped lips; any more, he thought, would've taken away from her natural beauty. She looked to be about six or seven inches shorter than him.

"Are you going to school tomorrow?" Jill asked.

"Yes. I enrolled earlier today."

"I saw your car out front. What a beauty! Will you be driving it?"

"I hope so. I saw several cars in the school parking lot, so I assume the students are allowed to drive their cars. Are they?"

"Yes, they are."

"How do you get to school?"

"I ride the school bus."

"Would you like to ride with me?"

"I'd love to."

"Your boyfriend won't mind?"

"I don't have a boyfriend. I guess I'm too much of a loner. Do you have a girlfriend?"

"No, I don't. I'm also a loner."

"From what Tom told Mom and me about your mother, I think you have a good reason for wanting to be alone."

Neither talked for a moment. "I won't deny," Jill said, "that I was uncomfortable when Tom told me you were going to be staying with us, but now that I've met you, I don't feel that way. I think we can become close friends."

"I hope so. I'd like that."

It only took a few days for Carl and Jill to become comfortable with each other and they were always together. She rode to and from school with him, and after school she helped him clean Tom's boat. And the weekends Tom's boat was chartered, and Carl was out fishing, she washed and polished *Blue*. He tried to get her to use *Blue* on the days he had to work, but she never did. She did enjoy using *Blue* when she and her mother went shopping.

They also went to football games and other school activities together, did their homework together, mowed and trimmed the yard together; they helped Joyce with cleaning the house, and occasionally helped prepare dinner. Carl enjoyed cooking, and often, on the days there was no school, he and Jill got up early and had breakfast ready for Tom and Joyce when they got up.

* * * *

"It smells like the girls have been busy," Tom said. It was Thanksgiving Day and he and Carl had just returned from a day in the Gulf. Tom had not wanted to charter his boat on the holiday, but the men who chartered it were regular customers, and he couldn't bring himself to refuse them.

Joyce and Tom kissed as soon as he entered the house. "Jill and I have everything cooked, so as soon as you fellows finish your showers, we'll be ready to eat."

Carl admired how Joyce always greeted her husband with a kiss, no matter how grimy he was or fishy he smelled.

Not since his father's death, had he allowed his mother to caress him. It seemed the only time she wanted to show affection was while intoxicated. He resented her insincere efforts and had always managed to avoid her.

When Tom and Carl returned to the dining room, the table was set and Joyce and Jill were positioning the last of the beautifully prepared food.

"I'm a lucky man," Tom said while embracing both Jill and her mother.

They kissed his cheeks. "We're lucky too."

When Carl saw Joyce's open arms and inviting smile, he rushed to her. "Thanks for letting me stay with you, and I appreciate everything you've done."

With her arms still around him, she said, "I want you to know that we really enjoy you being with us, and you're welcome to stay as long as you like."

"Thanks."

Jill was standing behind her mother, looking at Carl, and waiting her turn. He went to her, and with their cheeks together, and without saying a word, they held each other tightly. He couldn't help but notice that she relaxed her arms a little after he did.

Later that night Carl's mother called. "Hi, Son."

As soon as he heard her call him "Son," he knew she was intoxicated.

"I've moved in with Frank and I want to give you his phone number." After giving him Frank's number, she continued, "We're thinking about renting my house."

Carl cringed when she referred to his grandfather's house as hers. His grandfather willed it to Tom and his father. His father had purchased Tom's half from him for the appraised value—now she was calling it hers.

He asked her to let him know before she rented it so he could get the rest of his things. She said she would.

When Carl began making more money than it took to pay for his school lunches and supplies, insurance and gas for his car, and a few other necessities, he began paying Tom and Joyce room and board. They didn't want to take his money, but he insisted. What little money was left, he saved, and by Christmas he had enough for a few presents.

Jill was always with him when he went shopping, which made it difficult to buy something for her. They agreed that he would go alone one night to buy for her, and she would take *Blue* the next night and shop for him. On one of the nights they were together, he bought a small bottle of perfume for his mother. Jill tested it; she liked the smell, and he liked how it smelled on her.

Carl worked every day and both weekends during the two weeks school was out for Christmas vacation. He and Jill had made plans to drive to Fort Myers and visit his mother on Christmas day. He had called a few days earlier to let her know that he and Jill would be arriving Christmas morning. He hoped she would be sober.

"We'll be back early," Carl told Joyce. She had planned a large Christmas dinner for later that evening.

So that he and Jill could get an early start, Jill, Joyce, Tom, and Carl had opened their presents on Christmas Eve.

On the way to Fort Myers, and completely out of character, Jill talked continuously and about many things. She was nervous. He put a lot of effort into following what she was saying, but his mind was on his mother and what her condition would be when they arrived. He even wondered if Frank was going to be civil, or would he be angry and seeking revenge. He sensed that Jill was concerned about what he was thinking.

"Don't worry," she said. "There's nothing your mother can say or do that will affect our friendship."

Carl felt sick as he pulled in Frank's driveway. He took a few deep breaths, then looked over at Jill. "Are you sure you're ready for this?"

"I'm ready. But are you ready? You seem to be really nervous."

"I am nervous. I'm so nervous I'm almost sick. I just hope they're sober."

"It's ten o'clock. Surely they won't be intoxicated this early."

"I hope you're right."

Even before they reached the door, they heard Frank's voice coming from inside the dark house. "If you're looking for your mother, she's not here!"

Carl couldn't see him and was uncomfortable knowing he could see them. "Where is she?"

"I caught her with another man, so I kicked her out."

"So where is she?" Carl repeated.

"Damned if I know! Probably back at her house."

Without saying another word, Carl turned and, with Jill by his side, walked back to *Blue*. He opened her door and, while closing it, their eyes fixed on each other's. The sad look on her face, created an urge to lean in the window, take her beautiful face in his hands, kiss her gently on the lips, and say, "Let's go back to Naples." But he didn't and the urge passed.

"How far is your grandfather's house from here?"

When talking to Jill about his home in Fort Myers, he had always referred to it as his grandfather's house.

"Not far. About two miles." It was a long, quiet two miles.

Jill pointed to his house. "I'll bet that's your house…. Right?"

"That's it."

"Its color caught my attention first, since it's the only yellow, trimmed in white, house on the block. It's much bigger and more attractive than you described. I had no idea it was two-story. And look at those large, white columns around the front and side porches. It's a typical, old style, Florida home, like one you'd find in Key West, or some other community along the west coast of Florida."

"Evidently, my grandfather patterned it after the houses he'd seen while sailing up and down the coast."

"What do you mean?…Was he a sea captain?"

"Yes. My grandfather and his brother built two large schooners, then used them to haul freight and passengers from Cuba to New Orleans."

"Wow! What an interesting life they must've had. What were their names?"

"My grandfather was Captain Jack. His brother was Captain Bill."

"*Captain Bill* was the name of Tom's shrimp boat before he sold it and bought the charter boat he has now."

"I know. And *Captain Jack* was the name of my father's boat."

The house was located on a corner lot. The front faced Monroe Street; the side and two-car garage faced Victoria Avenue.

"I don't recognize this car," Carl said when he pulled beside the car parked in the driveway. "It probably belongs to the man Frank caught Mom with.... I have a bad feeling.... Would you prefer to wait in the car until I find out what's going on?"

"I'm OK."

Carl knocked, then opened the door. While holding the door open for Jill, he noticed that she had remembered to bring his mother's gift.

They were greeted by a mixture of smoke, whiskey, cheap perfume, and several other foul odors. The first thing that caught Carl's eye was the painting that hung over the mantle was missing. It wasn't just any painting; it was one he had patiently watched his father paint for him when he was ten years old. Now, the mantle, and even the room, looked bare.

While he looked around the living room for the picture, his mother staggered in.

"Hi, Son.... I guess Frank told you where to find me?" She looked down at the belt on her robe, as if tying it was more important than greeting her son or meeting his friend.

"He wasn't sure, but he thought you might be here.... Mom, I'd like you to meet Jill. Jill, this is my mother, Lois." Without giving them a chance to speak, he continued, "Where's Dad's painting?"

"I don't know. I guess the couple I let stay here took it," she calmly said.

"What couple?"

"A nice man and woman I met. They needed a place to stay for a few days, so I let them stay here."

"Where did you meet them, 'The Chicken Coop'?" The Chicken Coop was her favorite bar.

"I'm not sure. But I think it was."

He reached for Jill's hand. "We better check the rest of the house."

"Oh, no!" he screamed when he and Jill entered his room. "Not my cedar chest!...They took my cedar chest!"

He looked around his room, then at Jill, "I can't believe this.... My dad built that chest for me. He called it my 'secret chest,' and only I had the key. He told Mom that she was never to force me to open it for any reason, and he would do the same. Not only did it have things I had saved from when I was six years old, it contained many items of my father's that I had planned to keep forever. Things like his pocket knife, his paintings, his class ring, and even his boots and favorite hat."

Jill reached for him, but he put his hands over his face and sat on the edge of the bed without seeing her open arms. Jill sat beside him. She almost had her arm around him when he jumped up. "Oh my God!! My tools!!"

He clutched Jill's hand and almost dragged her to the garage. "Oh, God, please!" he pleaded when he opened the back door to the garage and saw the utility room door open.

He was speechless as he looked around the empty room. Then, while sitting on a stool, with his face in his hands, and his elbows resting on the workbench his father had built, he felt Jill's arm ease around him. He was comforted by her compassion, but wished he were alone. He wanted to cry.

"All my tools," he said, still holding his face in his hands. "But what's worse, they stole my father's tools…and my grandfather's. I was hoping to pass them on to my children, like my grandfather and father did."

Jill pulled him closer. "Maybe we can find them."

"Maybe. But I doubt it…. Let's go in and ask Mom what she knows about the man and woman she so graciously let stay in our home."

Carl's mother was sitting on the couch, drinking a beer, and smoking a cigarette. Her hair was in as much of a mess as when they first arrived.

"Do you have any idea where I can find the people you let stay here?" His voice trembled with anger.

"Why?" she asked, while blowing smoke out of one side of her mouth and high in the air.

"Why!" he shouted. "How can you ask, 'why!' They stole everything I own!"

"I don't know who they are. I only saw them that one night."

"How could you do that, Mom!" he shouted. "You didn't even know them!...The least you could've done is let me know so I could've gotten my stuff out!...Jesus Christ, Mom! What were you thinking!"

At the same time he smelled the rancid, aroma of a smoker's body odor, he saw Jill look past him. He turned and was face to face with a man he had never met. The man was large and hairy, wearing a pair of dirty jeans, with no shirt or shoes. He looked as if he had not bathed or shaved in at least a week.

Seeing the man leaning against the door opening with a silly smirk on his face only increased Carl's anger. He didn't think it was possible to be more upset than he was, but he was wrong.

The stranger straightened from his leaning position and approached Carl. His face was close, so close that the rank smell of his breath caused Carl to stop breathing.

"You can't talk to your mother like that!" the man shouted. "It's her house and she don't have to tell you a shit'n thing."

A rush of anger went through Carl like he had never experienced, and before he knew what he was doing, he grabbed the man's arm, twisted it behind his back, and shoved him against the wall.

"You're breaking my arm!" the man screamed.

While holding the man's arm with one hand, he grabbed him behind the neck with the other then forced him toward the door leading outside. Jill had the door open when he arrived.

He shoved the man off the porch and into the yard, then watched as the man tried to straighten his arm while face down on the cold grass.

"You can't leave me out here. It's cold," the man said when he managed to get in a sitting position.

"You poor, drunk bastard. Go get in your car."

When Carl returned, he just stood looking at his mother, waiting for her to say something. When she didn't, he extended his hand to Jill, and she gave him his mother's present.

"Merry Christmas, Mom."

She looked at the present, then to him. "I don't want your damn present. You think you can come in here, beat up my new boyfriend, talk to me disrespectfully, then give me a present and think I'll forgive you? You better think again."

Without taking his eyes off his mother, he handed her present to Jill.

"Good-bye, Mom." His voice was a little more than a whisper. "Let's get out of here."

Instead of leaving, they walked next door to see Ralph. After introducing Ralph and Jill, Carl asked Ralph if he had seen who had stayed at his house. Ralph said he saw some lights a few nights before, but thought it was Carl's mother. When Ralph heard what had happened, he blamed himself for not checking and could hardly control his anger. It took some time, but Carl finally convinced Ralph that it was not his fault.

It pleased Carl to know that Ralph had gotten his old job at the marina. Then, after getting each other caught up on all the things that had happened since he moved to Naples, he and Jill headed for the Sheriff Department to report his loss. The deputy assured him that a deputy would investigate the scene the next day and get back with him.

Before Carl arrived in Fort Myers, he told Jill he was going to show her where he had worked and many other points of interest, but after discovering that his cherished possessions were stolen, nothing seemed important.

* * * *

It seemed to Jill that getting home was most important, and she was pleased when Carl turned south on The Tamiami Trail. She realized that visiting the place he worked, and the other places he had said he wanted to show her, would have only brought him additional grief. Not knowing what to say, she fixed her eyes on the road ahead and listened to the only sound—*Blue's* purring engine.

Even though she was looking forward, she could see his hands gripping the top of the steering wheel, and by the squeaking sounds his hands made as they tightened and twisted, she knew he was thinking about his loss. Trying to distract him from his thoughts, she turned and looked at him. She felt certain her face conveyed the sorrow she felt when he slowly turned his head and returned her look.

When she saw his expressionless smile and the hurt in his eyes, she wished she could think of something to say. Unlike some, who felt the need to exaggerate their feelings until they had the suffering person in tears, she had never been comfortable discussing an unpleasant situation with someone who was trying to control their emotions.

It was a little past noon. Most people were home enjoying their family and preparing Christmas dinner. Jill wondered how Carl's thoughts were affecting him. She wished there was more traffic to distract him. *This Christmas will certainly be one I'll never forget.*

She wondered how many similar Christmas's Carl had endured.

He turned toward her, and when she turned to accept his look, she saw that he wasn't looking at her. He was looking at his mother's present on the seat between them. She watched as he slowly returned to looking ahead, then turned back, picked it up, and threw it out the window.

At that moment, it became important to let him know she cared, and she could no longer suppress her desire to comfort him. She moved closer and focused on the muscle in his jaw, tightening and relaxing. His eyes were glued to the road, but when she noticed that he was aware of her looking at him, she turned to face him even more. And when he smiled and lifted his arm, she slid beneath it and snuggled up close. They stayed that way, without talking, until they were in Naples.

Before they reached home, Jill moved back to her side of the car; neither wanted her mother or Tom to get the wrong impression.

Chapter 6

Several months passed before Carl forced himself to call his mother. When he did, the conversation was tense and short. She was still living at his grandfather's house, and she and Frank were in the process of getting a divorce. He wanted to ask if she had heard anything about his missing tools and other items, but avoided the question. Her answer would only upset him and cause him to lose his temper.

The stress of living in a new environment and always wondering if he was complicating Tom, Joyce, and Jill's lives was not easy, and knowing that each time the phone rang it could be his mother, added to his discomfort. He assumed it was only a matter of time before she would call with some kind of emergency situation—one requiring him or Tom to get involved. It was not a comforting thought to know that Tom, by bringing him into his home, was exposing his family to her selfish and inconsiderate actions.

Jill understood his concerns, and to help him cope and not have time to dwell on his situation, she did her best to keep him occupied.

Because Jill and Carl were always together, everyone at school assumed they were boyfriend and girlfriend. The boys didn't ask her out, and he was comfortable hanging out with her. They were attracted to each other and would have preferred to be more than just friends, but living together made that difficult. Whether it was work or play, they did it together, and she never tired of helping him clean Tom's boat after school. Carl looked forward to the weekends when only a few people chartered the boat. On those days, Jill joined Tom and him, and they enjoyed having her on board as much as she enjoyed being there.

Carl was amazed at how much Tom reminded him of his father, especially, at dinner. Dinner was a special time and, sometimes, lasted for hours. Tom never ran out of interesting stories about his and Carl's father's early youth and teenage adventures, but was careful not to dominate the conversation. He always asked Jill, her mother, and Carl, questions that stimulated them to comment on things of interest to them. Carl cherished those long dinners. Not only did they bring him closer to his new family, they brought him closer to his father.

One night in late January, while the four of them were cleaning up after dinner, the phone rang; it was Ralph. "Guess what?"

"I give up," Carl answered.

"I saw some of your dad's tools in the tool box of a boat carpenter who came to work on a boat in the marina."

"Is he still working there?"

"Yes. But you don't have to worry about rushing here to confront him."

"Why?"

"I called the Sheriff Department, and a deputy came and confiscated the tools. You'll never guess who the man said he bought them from."

"Who?"

"Your mother's husband."

"Frank Martello?"

"Yes.... It seems to me that he was trying to get even with you for beating his ass."

"You're probably right. Where is he?"

"A deputy took him to jail. He said he'll call you as soon as he questions him. But I just had to let you know."

"I'm glad you did. And thanks for calling the Sheriff. I'll let you know what the deputy says. Maybe Jill and I can drive up this weekend and pick up my stuff."

Soon after talking with Ralph, the deputy called. Frank had confessed and since there would not be a trial, there was no need to hold the stolen items for evidence. He could pick them up the following week. Carl's eyes filled with tears when the deputy said that when they searched Frank's house, they found the rest of the tools and his cedar chest with its lock intact and unopened. But what pleased him most was knowing his dad's painting was not damaged. *Ralph is right. Frank did it for revenge.*

It was Saturday of the following week before Carl and Jill could go to Fort Myers; Joyce suggested Saturday. She had often helped Tom with his charters before Carl came to live with them, and was looking forward to a day on the water.

Blue's trunk wasn't large enough for the cedar chest, so Tom suggested they take his pick-up truck.

Their first stop was the Sheriff Department. The deputies had retrieved everything Carl had reported missing. He thanked them, then he and Jill, with the deputies' help, loaded his prized possessions in Tom's truck and headed for the marina to visit Ralph.

Carl introduced Jill to his former boss and the other employees. Then after showing her the marina, and introducing her to many of the boat owners, they went to lunch with Ralph. They chose The Snack House Restaurant. The Snack House had been Carl and Ralph's favorite restaurant since they were twelve.

Carl was anxious for Jill to experience the atmosphere and the best hamburger in town.

"I'm impressed," Jill said after taking a bite of her burger. "I can see why you like eating here."

"I think if we'd had the money," Ralph said, "we would've eaten here every night. It's open twenty-four hours, seven days a week, and there were many times when we were here late at night. Several times until two in the morning."

"Didn't the police question why you were out that late?"

"Na.... Carl and I became good friends with most of them, and still are. They knew we were just getting away."

She understood why Carl would be out roaming the streets, but wondered why Ralph would. "Where were your parents?"

"My father died when I was two, my mother had to work all day and half the night to support my sister, brother, and me. She had it rough."

"I'll bet she did," Jill said. "She sounds like one helluva lady."

"She is."

There was one of those awkward moments of silence when no one knows what to say.

"Well, Ralph," Carl broke the silence, "what's Mom been up to?"

"Have you heard who she's dating?"

"No, I haven't."

"Do you remember the man who owned the lumber company where we used to play in that big pile of sawdust?"

"Sure. Don Pollard. He and Dad were good friends. I think they went to the same school.... Don's going with Mom!"

"I'm pretty sure. His car has been there for the last two weekends, and most nights during the week."

"I wonder how she trapped him? He's a 'cut above' her usual clients."

"Carl!" Jill said. "That was mean."

"I know, but he's a well-respected businessman, not the type man Mom is accustomed to dating.... Maybe she's changed? I doubt it, but maybe.... I hadn't planned to see her—I wanted to avoid a confrontation—but," he looked at Jill, "I guess we should stop by and check on her."

"I think we should."

His mother greeted them at the door. He was shocked. She looked sharp. Her slacks and shirt were pressed; her straggly hair he was accustomed to was cut and well groomed. Her makeup was not gaudy, as usual; she had on just enough to enhance her beautiful eyes and attractive face. There had been many times, before his father's death, she was told that she resembled Elizabeth Taylor.

Instead of the house being cluttered and dirty, as usual, it was clean and tidy. There was even the pleasant aroma of something cooking.

"Well, what a pleasant surprise," his mother said.

While embracing, he thought about the many years it had been since she last displayed affection while sober.

"Hi, Jill," she said as they hugged. "I'm so glad you stopped by."

Carl was first to see Don. He was wearing an apron and walking from the kitchen. He was much shorter than Carl remembered.

"Hi, Don. I'm Carl. I doubt if you remember me. I used to play in that large pile of sawdust and shavings in the back of your lumber company."

"Sure. I remember you. I always wanted to join you," he said while vigorously, shaking Carl's hand. "And this must be Jill?"

"Hi," Jill said.

He ignored her extended hand and wrapped his arms around her. "I've heard so much about you."

Carl glanced at his mother. She was smiling but would not return his look. Since she had only seen Jill once, he wondered what she had told Don. He figured she had fabricated something to make Don believe that she and Jill were close.

Don turned back to Carl. "Your mother and I are cooking a large pot of spaghetti, and we'd love for you and Jill to join us for dinner."

"Thanks, but we just had lunch, and we should be getting back to Naples." Carl was reluctant to accept.

"By the time the sauce is ready, you'll be hungry," Don persisted. "I really wish you'd stay. I have some plans for the house I'd like to go over with you."

"Plans for the house? This house?"

"Yes. Didn't your mother tell you that as soon as her divorce is final, we're getting married?"

"No. She didn't."

"Lois. I thought you said you told him."

"I thought I did…. Well, he knows now." She reached for Jill's hand. "Let's go check the sauce."

"We don't have to rush home," Jill said before leaving with Carl's mother. "And the sauce smells delicious."

Carl knew she was trying to help him feel comfortable with staying, which would give him and his mother an opportunity to spend some time together.

He turned his nose toward the kitchen and took a deep breath. "It does smell good....

You better call your mother and let her know we'll be a little late."

Carl chose his favorite chair. He was anxious to hear what Don meant when he said he had plans for the house.

Don removed his apron and sat in a chair close to his. Carl sensed that Don knew he was concerned.

"I can just imagine how shocked you were to hear that I want to make some changes to your home, especially, not knowing that your mother and I plan to marry. But, I want you to know, I won't make them if you prefer I don't."

"What kind of changes?"

"I have a home, and that's where we'll live, so I thought it would be a good idea to convert the upstairs into an apartment. That way we can rent the upstairs and the downstairs.... My heart is not in good shape, so if something happens to me, your mother will have some income. Even now she has some large debts that need to be paid. To pay for the remodeling and her debts, we will need to get a small mortgage. But the rent from the upstairs alone will take care of the mortgage."

"How much will the mortgage payments be?"

"I estimate about $40, no more than $45."

"I don't know, Don." The thought of a mortgage on his grandfather's house was not something he was comfortable with. "Can't she rent the whole house and let that money pay her debts?"

"Probably. But I have a fourteen-year-old son, and if, or when, I pass away, he'll inherit my house, and your mother will have to move back here. The rent from the upstairs apartment should provide her with a fairly good income."

"That's very considerate of you. But, I won't deny that I'm not pleased to know my grandfather's home will have a mortgage."

"I understand, but under the circumstances, I think it's best."

Carl leaned forward and placed his face in his hands; he was silent for a moment, then slowly raised his eyes from behind his hands. The words telling Don that he didn't agree with getting a mortgage, and he would prefer if he held off on the remodeling, were on the tip of his tongue, but instead, he asked, "How can I help?"

"I can't think of a thing. I've got it covered. But if something comes up that I feel you'd like to be involved with, I'll let you know."

As soon as Carl headed *Blue* home, he began to wonder if his decision to let Don and his mother get a mortgage on his grandfather's house was right.

"Don seems to be a really nice guy," Jill said.

"Yes he does. I just hope Mom doesn't create more problems than he can deal with."

"Let's think positive. She seems to be trying, and I believe it will help if we show our support. Maybe we should visit them more often?"

"Maybe."

"You still have your doubts, don't you?"

"I wish I didn't, but I do. As they say, 'A leopard can't change its spots.'"

"I realize you've had many years of grief while coping with a less than desirable mother, but now you have Don and me to help. So, let's be patient and give her a chance."

It pleased him to hear her say, "let's be patient." He wanted to show his affection, but knew he shouldn't. "I want you to know that I appreciate the effort you've made to understand my situation. You are the closest friend I've ever had."

"Even closer than Ralph?"

"Yes. Ralph and I are close, and have been for many years, but his and my friendship is more of a guy thing, whereas my feelings for you are much different. There are times, like now, when I want to take you in my arms and hold you until you beg me to let go."

She leaned toward him, put her head on his shoulder, and her arm over his waist. "I have a feeling you'd let go before I ask you to."

He lifted his arm, encouraging her to slide closer, and she did.

She kissed him on the cheek. "As much as I desire to be more than just your friend, and I know you feel the same, I just can't. There's no way we could hide our affection from Mom and Tom, which would cause them, and us, to be very uncomfortable."

"I agree. But I want you to know something."

"What?"

"I am very fond of you."

She squeezed his waist. "And I'm more than fond of you."

They were silent for several minutes.

Jill lifted her face from his chest. "I think, before we let our feelings get the best of us, we should agree to be close friends and nothing more."

"It's not what I prefer, but out of respect for your mother and Tom, I agree." He tightened his arm around her shoulder. "Maybe someday?"

She raised her face to his. "Maybe."

* * * *

Soon after her divorce was final, Carl's mother and Don were married, which was a few weeks after his and Jill's visit. He and Jill made an effort to visit them every two or three weeks, and during those visits, he became close friends with Don and Don's son, Donnie. Even though he was pleased with his mother's transformation, he had his doubts that her actions were sincere and treated her with caution. Jill, however, regarded her change as an honest effort to be accepted and looked forward to their time together.

It was the beginning of summer vacation when Don finished remodeling the house. Jill and Carl were there for the finishing touches. Donnie was also there helping his father. Donnie lived with his mother, but since there was no school, he had moved in with his father for the summer.

Don mentioned that both apartments had rented, even before they were finished. The tenants would be moving in the next day.

When they finished checking out the apartments, Don suggested they follow him to his house for lunch. Carl's mother met them at the door and, as usual, Jill and she embraced, and then, with no more than a casual glance toward Carl, she escorted Jill to the kitchen. From the strong smell of mouthwash, and the glassy look in her eyes, even though he was allowed only a brief look, he knew she had been drinking. As Don watched them walk to the kitchen, Carl saw his smiling face and eyes change to disappointment.

When Don left to use the bathroom, Carl moved closer to Donnie. "Your dad looks tired. Has he been working late?"

"No. Not really."

Carl wasn't sure Donnie was aware of his father's heart condition, but sensed that Don was uncomfortable about something. Carl continued, "He was probably under a lot of tension while doing the remodeling. Maybe, now that it's finished, he'll be able to relax a little more."

"Maybe. But I doubt it."

By the tone in Donnie's voice, it was clear to Carl that his mother was the reason.

"Has my mother been putting pressure on your dad to take her out dancing and partying?"

"Well..."

"I was afraid this would happen, but I don't know what I can do."

"I'm not worried about it. Dad said if things don't improve, he'd do something about it."

"I hope he doesn't wait too long."

Carl's mother was the only one comfortable during lunch. She thought of herself as "the life of the party." Her loud voice dominated the conversations—a maneuver Carl had witnessed many times. It was an attempt to conceal her drinking. It saddened him to see Jill's expression change from optimism to despair as the hope she had for his mother's recovery was dashed. The grief on Don's face told it all: Not only had his efforts to help not been appreciated, he had exposed his son to an undesirable situation.

For Carl and Jill, it was another long, silent ride home. Neither knew what to say.

Chapter 7

It was a little more than two weeks after Carl and Jill's disappointing visit with his mother when Donnie phoned. His father had suffered a heart attack and was in the hospital. It was too late to leave that evening, so Carl told Donnie that he and Jill would see him the next morning. It was still summer vacation and no school.

Their first stop was Don's home. Donnie was dressed and ready to go; Carl's mother was still in bed. She told them to go on to the hospital without her; she wanted to call Don's doctor and would be there later.

"Well," Carl said when he entered Don's room, "you look better than I expected."

"Hi, guys!" He put down what he was reading and lifted his arms to Jill. Their embrace was long.

"You don't look as if there's anything at all wrong with you," Jill said.

"What seems to be the problem?" Carl asked while they shook hands.

"I began having some severe chest pains. So my doctor decided to admit me for observation and run some tests."

Jill was close and holding his hand. "Do you know the results of the tests?"

"Some. I'll know more this afternoon…. The doctor said that no matter what the additional tests reveal, he has seen enough to know I'll have to have complete bed rest for several weeks."

"Here, or home?" Jill asked.

"At home.... I'm told I should be able to leave in two or three days."

By Don having a private room, visiting hours, or the number of visitors, was not enforced. But when Don's lunch was served, and to give him some privacy, Carl, Jill, and Donnie agreed to go get something to eat and return later in the afternoon.

Jill suggested The Snack House, and then suggested they stop and see if Carl's mother would like to join them.

"She's here," Carl said when he saw Don's car in the driveway. "I'll go in and ask if she wants to go. I'll be right back."

She was sitting at the kitchen table, in her housecoat, drinking a cup of coffee. "Hi, Mom. Did you call Don's doctor?"

"Yes, I did!"

By her expression he knew she was lying. But the many years of witnessing her irate, temper tantrums when someone questioned her, caused him to refrain from accusing her of not calling the doctor. "What did he say?"

"He said Don's faking, and for me not to worry."

"If his doctor feels that way, why did he put him in the hospital?"

"To pamper him."

"To pamper him! Why would he want to pamper him?"

"He's been Don's doctor for many years, and he doesn't want to lose the income."

"How can you believe that? You knew Don had a heart condition before you married."

"I think he made up his heart condition so I would feel sympathetic and wait on him hand and foot."

"I can't believe you think Don's faking. Look at all he's done for you. He didn't have to remodel our house. He did it so you would have an income if something happened to him."

"He did that for himself. He wants the extra income."

"I can see that nothing I say will change your mind. But, no matter what you think, please help him through this."

"As usual, you never think of your own mother!" In an effort to mask her lies and legitimize her comments, she began to shout. "Now it's Don!

Don! Don! What about my life! Do you think I'm going to stay home, knowing he's faking, and take care of him?"

She kept her distance so he couldn't smell the whiskey on her breath, but by her comments, and the way her words were slurred, he knew she had been drinking.

"It wouldn't hurt," he said, "if for once in your life you show a little compassion. Don deserves at least that."

"You think you're so smart! Don deserves nothing!"

Carl opened the door leading out, then stopped and looked back. "Unfortunately, you have convinced yourself that Don is using you, and, as usual, that's your way of justifying your selfish actions. But no matter how you feel, please, at least for a few weeks, be considerate and encourage him to get the rest the doctor said he needs. Show a little sympathy, especially, in Donnie's presence."

"Yeah! Yeah! Yeah! I'm always the one who takes care of everyone. No one ever thinks about what I need."

"Jill and Donnie are waiting for me, so I better be going. Oh! Jill wants me to ask if you'd like to join us for lunch?"

"No! I'm better off here, alone."

Carl tried to disguise his anger when he joined Jill and Donnie, but by the way Jill looked at him, he knew she was aware that his visit with his mother had not gone well.

"She didn't want to join us?" Donnie asked.

"Na. She has some other plans."

Instead of discussing what was said, both Carl and Jill concentrated on talking with Donnie on their way to The Snack House.

Before returning to the hospital, and after stopping by the marina to visit Ralph, they did some shopping. Jill picked out the perfect card and bought a small flower arrangement.

It was after three o'clock when they arrived at the hospital. Carl wondered if his mother had visited while they were away, but didn't ask. Jill, with her captivating personality, had Don laughing and carrying on as if he didn't have a problem.

After several hours, and even though Jill was holding his hand and doing her best to keep him cheered up, Don's face and eyes began to show concern. His smile was not as sincere, and he continually glanced toward the door. It was obvious that he was wondering where his wife was.

"I smell food," Donnie said, then looked out the door. "Yep. They're pushing the cart toward your room."

"Where did the time go?" Jill asked. "I think it'll be best if we let you eat in peace. Where should we go, guys? Back to The Snack House?"

"Sounds good to me," Donnie agreed.

Don squeezed Jill's hand. "I wish I could join you. I love The Snack House."

Jill leaned down, kissed him on the forehead, and whispered, "I wish you could too."

"Have you seen your mother?" were Don's first words to Carl when they returned.

Carl looked at the clock—7:00 PM. "She hasn't been to see you?"

"Not yet. The last time I saw her was last night. And then only…"

Carl turned to see what distracted Don. It was his mother, and she was with two other ladies. The room instantly reeked with the smell of cheap perfume.

While his mother made her way to Don's bed, Carl checked out the other women. They all, including his mother, had on extremely tight, low-cut dresses and were wearing way too much makeup to visit someone in a hospital. They looked cheap, sleazy, and gaudy.

He heard his mother talking to Don, but was not paying attention to what she said; the ladies looked familiar, and he was trying to remember where he had seen them. Then—like a blow to the stomach—he remembered.

He didn't take his eyes off the ladies while his mother introduced them to Don, Jill, and Donnie. "These are my friends, Ruby and Helen." He became even more uncomfortable when she put her arm around him and said, "And this is Carl. Hasn't he grown?"

"Yes he has," one of them said. "I'm sure you don't remember us, do you?"

"Yes I do," he said. Their smiles disappeared and everyone was silent. When his mother saw he was glaring at them, she removed her arm from around him and returned to Don.

"Since you're in good hands here, and there's not much I can do to help, Helen, Ruby, and I have decided to go to the Chicken Coop and do some dancing." Without giving Don a chance to answer, and seeing the situation between her friends and Carl was about to get ugly, she said, "I love you." Then kissed him on the forehead, waved to the others, and followed Helen and Ruby to the door. "I'll see you tomorrow."

Silence, and the sickening smell they left behind, filled the room. Carl saw Don's anger building. "I think Mom and those ladies have been friends for a long time. I guess it's been a while since they last spent some time together."

Don looked away from him. "I know who they are."

Carl realized that his effort to comfort Don and lessen his anger was in vain. The minutes that followed were uncomfortable for all. No one spoke.

"Guys," Don said. "…I know you mean well, but if you don't mind, I'd really like to be alone."

Donnie hugged his father without saying anything.

"I understand," Carl said. "We'll see you when you're home."

Jill kissed him on the lips. "Goodbye," she said, then wiped her tears from his cheeks.

"You acted as if you were uncomfortable being around Ruby and Helen," Jill said when Donnie was no longer with them and they were on their way back to Naples.

"I was."

She was silent as she watched his hands grip and twist the top of his steering wheel. After a few minutes, her curiosity got the best of her. "Why did those women upset you?" He didn't answer, but she could tell he was building up to it.

The sound of his hands twisting the steering wheel intensified.

"They're whores."

"How do you know that?" she asked.

He paused, then without taking his eyes off the road, he began: "During the War, World War II, they were Mom's closest friends. My dad was in the Navy, stationed on a ship far out in the Pacific. One night, when I was only six, I woke to a strange noise. I eased out of bed and went looking for its source. I can still remember how scared I was as I slowly opened my bedroom door and stepped out into the long, dark hallway. The noise seemed to be coming from the living room, so I cautiously tiptoed in that direction. There must've been a light on, or a full moon, because when I arrived, I saw two people on the couch. At the time, I didn't know what they were doing.

"I moved closer. 'Mom?' I asked. 'No,' was the answer I got.... It was Ruby. I could still hear the noise, so I continued searching. When I walked out onto the porch, I saw two people on our metal glider. It was the source of the noise. I stood beside them and watched for a while. I couldn't tell if it was Mom, so I asked, 'Mom?' Again, 'No.' was my answer...It was Helen.

"Now, not only was I scared, I was confused. As I made my way back down the hall toward my bedroom, Mom's bedroom door opened. The hall filled with light, and there, standing beside my naked mother, was a naked man. I had seen the man earlier that day in his Army uniform. Instead of finding something to cover her naked body, or being sympathetic and ask if something had scared me, or if I was sick, she scolded me for being up, then told me to go to my room and get back in bed."

"My God, Carl! No wonder you were shocked to see Ruby and Helen. But, how did you recognize them?"

"I'll never forget Ruby and her bright, red hair, or Helen and her jet-black hair. I wish I could forget them, but I'm afraid I never will. During the War, they always seemed to be with Mom, and the three of them were always with soldiers."

While looking straight ahead, as if in a trance, Jill said, "I can imagine that seeing your mother naked with another man, and him naked also, had to be a traumatic experience. One I'd hate to have."

"I've had many flashbacks of my youth, but that night returns to haunt me more often than the others. The shock of discovering that Mom was cheating on Dad is probably the reason.... When I recall that night, it's as if I'm overhead looking down at this scared little boy, tiptoeing in an eerie hallway toward a strange sound, looking for his mother. I don't view the experience through the eyes of the little boy—that would be too painful. Evidently, to reduce the pain, my mind chooses to view that night from a distance. It's trying to suggest that being on the outside looking in will be less disturbing. The only problem is: it doesn't work. I still feel the hurt."

"I overheard Tom tell Mom that the night your father died, he had discovered your mother was cheating on him, but I had no idea she had cheated many times before.... How could your father live with her?"

"He never knew."

"He never knew! Why didn't you tell him?"

"I don't know. I guess I was afraid it would hurt him.... You have no idea how many times I came close to telling him.... I wish I had.... If you only knew how much I wish I had."

Jill moved closer to him and, as usual, he lifted his arm and she snuggled beneath it. "Thanks for telling me," she said without looking up. "I've always thought the reason you have little or no respect for your mother is because of her drinking. Now I understand."

✳   ✳   ✳   ✳

It was a hot, humid Saturday night in July, and Carl couldn't sleep. The soothing, purr of the slowly turning ceiling fan usually lulled him to sleep, but not this night. Earlier, Jill, Joyce, and Tom had surprised him with a small birthday party—it was his seventeenth.

While wondering if the large amount of cake and ice cream was the reason he couldn't sleep, it dawned on him that for the first time since his father's death, he was experiencing love. Not only did he love his new family, he felt their love.

He was still listening to the fan and staring at the ceiling when he heard the phone ring, and soon after, there was a knock on his door. It was Tom. "Donnie's on the phone."

"Donnie?"

Tom didn't answer. Carl looked at the clock—1:00 AM. *It's got to be something serious for Donnie to call at this time of night.*

It had been more than two weeks since he and Jill were in Fort Myers. He had phoned Donnie several times to inquire about Don's condition; Donnie had assured him that his father was getting the much-needed rest his doctor had insisted he get.

"Donnie! What's wrong?"

Donnie was crying hysterically, and after several attempts, he finally was able to say: "Dad is dead."

"Dead!"

"Yes. The ambulance is just now taking him away."

"I thought he was getting better. What happened?"

"Your mother and Dad were having an argument when he just fell to the floor."

"Why were they arguing at this time of night?"

"She left about seven o'clock to go dancing, or somewhere. Dad told her he wasn't feeling well and asked her to stay, but she left. I tried to keep him in bed, but he began pacing the floor and cussing. It was about twelve o'clock when I finally got him back in bed. Soon after, your mother came home. I was in my room and could hear them talking, screaming at each other is more descriptive. By the way your mother was talking, I knew she had been drinking. I heard a loud bump, and then there was silence.

"Your mother came into my room and said, 'I think your father's dead.' I ran to him, he wasn't breathing, so I called an ambulance, and then his doctor. The doctor arrived in just a few minutes. When he took a blanket off the bed and placed it over my dad, I knew he had passed away."

Carl felt a hand on his shoulder. "Let's go," he heard Jill say. He looked up and saw tears flowing down her cheeks, onto her lips, then dripping off her trembling chin.

"Have you called your mother?" Carl asked.

"No. My mother and stepfather are out of town and won't be back until tomorrow afternoon."

"Where's Mom?"

"She's in the kitchen. Do you want me to get her?"

"That's OK. I'll talk with her when Jill and I get there. We're leaving now. We should be there in about forty-five minutes. Hang in there, Donnie."

"I will, and thanks for coming."

"Where's your mother?" Jill asked when he hung up the phone.

"In the kitchen. Probably pouring herself another glass of courage."

"Let's hurry!" she said while rushing to her room to dress.

Tom put his arm around Carl. "Except for being there for Donnie, there's not much you and Jill can do, so don't speed and be careful."

"I will."

There was a car parked along the curb in front of Don's house.

"I wonder whose car that is?" Carl said.

"Could be the doctor's."

"Maybe? But I doubt if a doctor would drive a car in that bad of condition."

Even though it was close to two o'clock in the morning, Donnie was standing by the driveway, waiting for them. *Blue* had barely stopped when he opened Jill's door and fell into her arms. They held each other and wept for several minutes.

Listening to the grief in Donnie's voice and seeing how sympathetic Jill was, had Carl's throat so tight he was afraid to talk.

"Where's Mom?" he forced out.

"In the house," Donnie sobbed.

"Is she displaying any remorse?"

"She didn't cry a tear until that man arrived. Now she's bawling like a baby."

"What man?"

"The man who owns that car. I don't know who he is. He just showed up."

Carl's grief quickly turned to anger. "You and Donnie wait here. I'll be right back."

A man was sitting on the couch holding his mother while she wailed. "Oh, Son! I want you to meet a dear friend.... Eddie, this is my son, Carl."

Eddie stood and extended his hand. "Nice meeting you."

Carl, reluctantly, shook his hand, then asked, "How long have you known my mother?"

"A couple days."

"You and my mother have been dating while her husband was too sick to get out of bed?"

"I didn't know he was sick."

"Why are you here tonight?" Carl asked.

"Your mother called to tell me her husband died, and asked me to come over. She seemed really upset, so I came to comfort her."

"By the looks of the clothes on the floor, if I hadn't walked in when I did, there would've been a lot more than comforting going on."

Carl's mother reached for Eddie's hand and pulled him down beside her. Eddie looked up at Carl. "It's not what you think."

"Yeah. Sure it's not.... This is not a good time for you to be here, so I would appreciate it if you'd leave."

"I'm not leaving until your mother asks me to."

"Mom is not going to ask, so I'm telling you. You have about a minute to get your shoes on and leave. Otherwise, I'm going to put you in that piece of junk out front without opening the door." While standing as close to Eddie as he could without touching him, he looked down at him and asked, "Is there any part of what I said you don't understand?"

"Don't leave me, Eddie. You have no idea how mean he'll be to me if you go."

"I think it would be best if I leave." He leaned forward and picked up his shoes, socks, and shirt, and then, without putting on his shoes, walked out the door without saying another word.

"Mom.... I know you're too drunk to understand much of what I'm going to say, but I'm going to say it anyway. I'm going to pour every drop of liquor that's in the house, down the drain. You're going into your room and stay there until you're sober. I don't want Jill to see you in this condition."

"Jill's with you?"

"Yes. Now pick up your clothes and get in your room before she comes in."

She hurriedly, picked up her clothes, went to the bathroom, and then to her bedroom. He was pleased to see she didn't want Jill to see her intoxicated and nearly undressed.

Soon after he poured out her whiskey, and several other kinds of booze, Jill and Donnie joined him.

"Where's your mother?" Jill asked.

"She's in her room."

While waiting for Carl, Jill had heard his assertive voice, saw the man come out of the house, and watched him, while holding his shoes and clothes, cautiously tiptoe through the prickly grass to his car. She knew there was more to the story but didn't ask.

They stayed with Donnie until early morning; that's when he asked if they could take him home. Carl and Jill didn't want to leave him alone, so they took him to breakfast, then to the marina to inform Ralph of Don's death. Sunday was the marina's busiest day, so there was enough happening to help distract Donnie from thinking about his loss. It was later in the afternoon when they took him home. They waited with him until his mother arrived.

It was sad for Carl and Jill to watch and listen to Donnie relive the night of his father's death as he told his mother and stepfather. Afterwards,

Donnie's mother told Carl she would get with his mother to discuss the funeral arrangements.

Carl and Jill stopped by to see how his mother was doing. She was in her room. But, by the smoke still lingering in the living room, they knew she had recently gone to her room. Probably, they thought, when she saw them drive up. They figured she was suffering with guilt and a bad hangover. There was nothing they could do, so they headed *Blue* back to Naples.

Chapter 8

It was a few days after Don's funeral when Carl received a phone call from Donnie's mother: "I hate to bother you with this, but your mother is becoming a real pain in the ass.... Since Don didn't have an opportunity to change his will, she's contesting it. The will clearly states that Donnie is to inherit his father's house. But, her attorney has informed us that since her name was not mentioned in Don's will, she gets the house."

"How can that be?" Carl asked. "Everyone, including me, knew Don had planned to leave his house to Donnie."

"I know. I've tried to talk with her, but she won't even discuss our concerns on the phone, much less in person. She said her attorney will answer my questions, and I should call him."

"Have you called him?"

"Yes. He said that not only will she get the house, she'll get his car, boat, and half, if not all, of everything else Don owned. Thank God he had enough foresight to transfer his share of his and his brother's lumberyard into his brother's name, or something like that. I don't know the details, but, at least, it's protected."

"I'm so sorry. I wish I could say she'll be considerate and do the right thing. But, unfortunately, that's not her style. There are only two days left of summer vacation, so tomorrow will be my last opportunity to talk with her. Maybe I can change her mind."

"I was hoping you'd say that."

"I'll do my best, but don't get your hopes up. My mother is very stubborn."

"I'm finding that out."

When Carl told Jill what his mother was doing, she suggested he go to Fort Myers alone; she felt he would have more success if she was not with him. Since he didn't know how involved his visit would be, or how long it would take, he agreed.

A shiny new pickup truck was in Don's driveway, so Carl had to park *Blue* in front of the house next to the curb. He didn't have to wait long before he discovered who owned the truck—Eddie met him at the door.

"Is that your truck?" Carl asked.

"Yes, it is. Isn't she a beauty?"

Carl looked at him suspiciously without answering.

"I needed a new truck for my business…. Your mother's in the bathroom. She'll be out in a minute."

"What kind of business do you have?"

"The garbage business."

"The garbage business! What do you mean, 'the garbage business?'"

"I'll be picking up the trash and garbage of those living in the rural areas."

"So, you're not in business yet."

"Not yet, but, with your mother's help, it won't be long."

He was about to ask Eddie what he meant, when he heard, "Hi, Son. What brings you to town?" There was that familiar "son" and the smell of mouthwash; he knew she had been drinking.

"I came to talk with you."

"About what?"

"Can we talk in private?"

She sat on the couch next to Eddie and put her arm around him. "No. I want Eddie here. Eddie and I don't have any secrets, especially now that we're partners in a new business he's starting."

"I heard," Carl said while looking at Eddie. When he realized Eddie wasn't leaving, not even the room, he asked, "Where's the money coming from?"

"What do you mean 'where's the money coming from!' You know I have money! I've always had money! You know that!"

He had seen this act a hundred times before—she was trying to impress Eddie.

It was not the ideal time to ask about Don's house, but he had no choice: "I understand, from talking with Donnie, that you plan to stay in his house for a while."

Her eyes became glassy and her mouth tightened and wrinkled. She stared at him for a moment. "This is my house!" she shouted. "Not Donnie's! And I don't know why he thinks it's his! His mother is the one putting those thoughts in his head! She's trying to get everything I own! And I don't understand why she feels I should part with something that's rightfully mine. If she wants Donnie to have a house, she can buy him one! But she can't have this one."

Carl realized, as usual, she had convinced herself that she was right, and getting her to believe something different was futile. Her lack of compassion didn't surprise him; he had heard similar comments all his life. But this time was different; it was Donnie who was the recipient of her inconsiderate abuse, and by ignoring her and walking away, like he normally did, would not help Donnie. He had to try.

"Mom, you have to be aware of Don's desire to have his son inherit his home. He even told me. And besides, his original will states it. That's why he converted our home into apartments. He told me that if he died, Donnie would inherit this home and you'd move back to our home. He said the rent from the upstairs would pay the mortgage and still have money left over. I doubt if he thought he would die before the mortgage was paid off. But even if he did, he left you with more than you had."

"He left me with more than I had! He left me nothing! If it hadn't been for the money I've saved all these years, I wouldn't have anything. I even had to help him pay his bills! Not only did I have to support him, I let him talk me into getting a mortgage on my house, which, by the way, was debt free. I'm sure you think the money went to the remodeling, but it didn't. Most of it went to Don's bills. Yeah, he left me with something all right. He left me with a mortgage to pay."

If there was any chance at all to help Donnie, he had to be patient and not interfere with her desire to impress Eddie. Even though he had an almost uncontrollable desire to expose her, he had no choice but to endure her deception. The many years of being conditioned to never dispute her, which gave credibility to her lies, prevented him from challenging anything she said. If he did, the conversation would be over.

"Please, Mom, don't let a technicality prevent Donnie from inheriting his father's house. You know it's what Don wanted. And it's not like you don't have a place to live; you have a perfectly good home. So please do what's right and let Donnie have his home."

"You are never on my side! You always side with those who want to steal from me.... I was the best thing that ever happened to Don. I tolerated his lies, let him mortgage my home to pay his debts, took care of him when he was sick, and now you want me to give a fourteen-year-old boy what I've earned! I can't believe you don't understand what I've had to endure. This is my home, and, according to my attorney, I can live here until I die. And there's nothing Donnie and his greedy mother can do about it."

"I tried," Carl said when he met with Donnie and his mother.

They had spent most of the morning with their attorney. He confirmed that by Don not changing his will, Carl's mother had a lifetime estate, which gave her the right to live in Donnie's house for as long as she pleased, or until her death. All that was required of her was she had to pay the taxes.

It was difficult for Carl to deal with the fact that his mother and a technicality were preventing Donnie from having the home his father wanted him to have. He could only imagine the disappointment, grief, and anger Donnie was experiencing. He believed the only word to accurately describe what Donnie felt was: "cheated."

"There's something else," Donnie's mother continued. "I knew Don had an insurance policy; he had it while we were married. Donnie was the beneficiary. When I called the insurance company, to inform them of Don's death, I was told he changed the beneficiary from Donnie to your mother. I wondered why he would do that? But, knowing him, he probably thought since Donnie was getting the house, she should have something. Now, I find out Donnie's not getting the house or the insurance."

"What was the value of the insurance?" Carl asked.

"Ten…thousand…dollars."

"Ten thousand dollars!…Now I understand why she's acting so wealthy."

"She doesn't have the money yet."

"She has plenty," Donnie said.

"Why do you think that?" Carl asked.

"While I lived with them, I saw my father's check book. It had more than two thousand in it, and your mother's name was on the account. Her name was also on his savings account; there was more than three thousand in it."

"Oh…my…God!" Donnie's mother said, then fell in a chair, put her hands over her face, and wept.

"I wish there was something I could do, but I know my mother, and you'll never see a penny. I hate to say that, but it's true."

"We have, pretty much, come to that conclusion," Donnie said. "The best we can hope for is she marries a man with a home, and she moves in with him."

"You are probably right," Carl agreed. "Let's hope it's soon."

Carl didn't even visit Ralph; he preferred to be alone. He drove by his grandfather's home, which only increased his sorrow. The yard was neglected, something he had never seen. He thought how disappointed his grandfather would be.

Not knowing where to go, or what to do, he let his emotions guide him. It wasn't long before he found himself sitting beside his favorite piling, on the end of the longest dock, at the City Yacht Basin. It had been his special place to be when the situation at home became too difficult to deal with. He had spent many hours on that very spot.

Hardly ever was there a boat tied to that part of the dock. It was far from the facilities.

Normally, traffic on the Caloosahatchee River was not heavy, but, day or night, there always seemed to be a few boats.

The clearance of the bridge crossing the river, The Edison Bridge, was low, so it had to open for almost all boats. During the last four years, Carl had become good at judging the size of the boat by the sound of its horn when it signaled for the bridge to open. The small boats had horns that were blown by mouth, which were difficult to hear. The larger boats had electric horns, which were louder, but similar to automobiles. But the ones that impressed him the most were the air horns on the larger boats and the tugboats. There were times when the blasts of an air horn coming from the other side of the bridge, where he couldn't see, stimulated his curiosity to the point of excitement.

The bridge would open, then he would patiently wait to see what boat came through. It could be a large, private yacht, such as the *Chanticleer*, Ralph Evinrude and Frances Langford's 118' yacht, which frequently docked at the yacht basin. Or, more often than not, it was a tugboat, pushing one or more large barges. Whatever the boat, he watched with admiration until the bridge was lowered.

Even at home, which wasn't far from the yacht basin, the sounds of the boat horns allowed him to imagine he was sitting on the dock watching the bridge open and close. He would visualize a boat, choose its direction, east or west, and choose its size. Picturing himself on the dock, alone, watching the boats, and listening to their sounds, would temporarily take his mind off his problems and brought him a little comfort—especially, at night.

Although it was a cool, summer day and the boats were many, his thoughts were not about the day or the boats. He was thinking about his mother and how cruel she was to Donnie. He wanted to help Donnie, but felt as if his hands were tied. He wondered how many times his friends and family had felt the same about him.

Even though he knew it would be a waste of time, the urge to drive back to Don's house and demand she do the right thing was hard to resist. There had been many who tried to reason with her, including him, but no one ever succeeded. *This time will be no different.*

A loud blast of an air horn, coming from the other side of the bridge, distracted him from his thoughts, as had happened many times before. Was it a tugboat pushing a barge or several barges, a large yacht, or a shrimp boat? He wondered.

As the bridge opened, he felt his excitement building. He never knew why, but was glad it did. Soon, two large barges, secured tight together, slowly made their way through the open span; both pushed by a humongous seagoing tugboat with black smoke gushing from its twin exhaust pipes. The intensity of the smoke signified that the captain had increased speed for better maneuverability. As Tom would say, "He's pouring the coal to her!"

Since the Edison Bridge was the last bridge before entering the Gulf, Carl knew the crew would soon have to separate the barges, add towlines between them and between the tug and the lead barge. The changes were usually made right out in front of where he was sitting. He was disappointed when the captain chose to keep steaming downriver until they were closer to the Gulf.

With nothing more of interest to occupy his mind, his thoughts returned to his mother and Eddie. There was no doubt in his mind that Eddie was a con artist. *When Don's money's gone, Eddie will be too. And it's a waste of time to try and convince her of Eddie's intentions.*

Normally, while at his special place, he was there to figure out how to solve a problem that affected him, but this time was different—it wasn't his problem. He had always convinced himself that if he was patient, his situation would get better, and it usually did. But Donnie's situation was more complicated. It would take many years, he figured, before Donnie could move into his father's home. "She'll probably die there," Carl said out loud for only the seagulls to hear.

A helpless feeling swelled inside him. Not only did he feel sorry for Donnie, he felt ashamed to be his mother's son. As he made his way off the dock, he told himself he didn't care if he ever saw her again.

While opening *Blue's* door, he heard another air horn. He looked toward the bridge but continued to open the door. He sat for a minute, looking at the bridge and his special place, then started *Blue's* engine. "Let's go home."

Chapter 9

During the next eight months, Carl called his mother two times, Mother's Day and Christmas; she was intoxicated both times. He would have preferred not to call, but, somehow, felt compelled to. Their conversations were short, but long enough to know she had not changed. Her selfish thoughts were the same, and she had no intention of letting Donnie take possession of his father's house. Both times he called, he wished he hadn't.

There was one month left of Jill and Carl's senior year when Jill met and began dating John Stevens. John had graduated the year before. To Carl, John seemed to be nothing but a con artist. He figured Jill would soon see through John's deception, but he was wrong. She assumed that since John was a minister's son, whatever he said was the truth. Carl wanted to expose John's lies, but felt she would resent his efforts.

Carl had always assumed that he would be Jill's escort for the senior prom, but when he discovered John was to be her date, he realized Jill's relationship with John was more serious than he had imagined. It bothered him. Not because he was jealous, he had always looked forward to Jill meeting someone special; it was because she refused to see the real John.

Ralph and Carl had often talked about joining the Navy. So, a few weeks after he and Ralph graduated, they talked with a Navy Recruiter. They signed up and were scheduled to leave the middle of July.

That evening, while having dinner, and after discussing his new adventure, Jill had a surprise of her own. She and John were getting married.

Joyce was beaming with delight as she and Jill leaned across the corner of the table and hugged. "John is a fine boy," Joyce said, "and I'm sure you'll be happy." She pulled away, but continued to hold Jill's hand.

Tom returned Carl's disappointed look with a concerned look of his own. They both had doubts about John. They realized John's charm and cunning ways had won over Jill and her mother, but they were not about to reveal their true thoughts and concerns. The apprehension they felt lessened when they heard Joyce ask, "You aren't planning to marry any time soon, are you?"

"We were hoping for sometime in September, but now that Carl is leaving in July, and I want him to be at the wedding, maybe we should have it before he leaves."

"That's too soon," Tom said. "Take your time. If you really love each other, it won't hurt to wait a little longer."

"You don't care much for John, do you?" Jill asked.

"I didn't say that. I just don't think marriage should be rushed."

"Tom is right," Joyce said. "If the love you and John have is strong, marriage can wait. Besides, we need time to plan it. I'm sure his father will want to perform the ceremony and have the wedding in his church. And that all takes time to prepare."

"You're right," Jill said. She looked down at her plate and, with her fork, began maneuvering her food around, then slowly looked up at Carl. "When do you get your first leave?"

"I get fourteen days after boot camp. Boot camp lasts nine weeks."

She did some quick, mental figuring. "That means you'll be home the last of September or the first of October. So, let's plan the wedding for the first Saturday in October. OK?"

Everyone agreed.

"Now that we have a date for Jill's wedding figured out," Tom said, "what are you going to do with *Blue* while you're in the Navy?"

"I don't know. I haven't thought about *Blue*."

"I have an idea. Let's go outside and talk about it." They were barely outside when Tom said, "God, I hope she's not making a big mistake!"

"Me, too."

"Are we the only ones able to see what a jerk John is?"

"It looks that way."

"Maybe we're misreading him."

"Maybe," was all Carl could say. He wanted to confirm that John was not only a jerk, he was dishonest, disrespectful, and self-centered, but didn't want to contribute to Tom's doubts.

"I think it'll be best," Tom said, "if we keep our thoughts to ourselves. If we offer an unfavorable opinion of John, Jill and her mother will think we're being negative and accuse us of thinking no one is good enough for her.... I realize dating a girl while living with her parents is not easy, but Joyce and I have always hoped that when you and Jill graduated, and you were out on your own, you and she would date, fall in love, and marry."

"I feel we would've if John hadn't come into the picture.... I love Jill, and I don't mean like a sister. There have been many nights I have laid awake, wishing I were in her arms. She told me she's had similar thoughts. But, out of respect for you and Joyce, we agreed to not allow ourselves to become romantically involved. Now that I know how you and Joyce felt, I wish we had dated and kept it from you."

"I wish you had too."

"I regret so much that smooth-talking John came along and swept her off her feet. And now she's making wedding plans. It hurts to know I've lost her, especially to an imbecile.... I'm sorry. I didn't mean to call him that. I guess I'm just jealous."

"Hopefully, she'll come to her senses before the wedding. If not," Tom smiled before continuing, "I guess I'll just have to learn to like the imbecile."

They laughed out loud for a moment before Carl changed the subject. "What do you think I should do with *Blue?*"

Tom pointed to his two-car garage. "I think you should leave her right here. Right next to Joyce's car. It won't hurt my old truck to stay out in the weather."

"Are you sure? I'd hate to know your truck is in the weather while *Blue's* in the garage."

"I know how close you are to your car, and I'll feel better if she's safe and sound in the garage. And, don't worry. I won't let the im…I mean John, drive her."

"Thanks."

Two days before Carl was scheduled to leave for the Navy, Jill surprised him by asking if she could go with him to Fort Myers and drive *Blue* back. He had planned to take the bus.

"What does John think of this?" He asked without suggesting John join them.

"He's not pleased, but he'll get over it."

The reason Carl had not asked her was because he thought John would resent not being invited, and he definitely was not going to ask him. John riding in *Blue* was bad enough, but the thought that he might convince Jill to let him drive, was unimaginable. To Carl, *Blue* was sacred—only Ralph, Jill, and he had experienced driving her, and that's the way he preferred to keep it.

Carl and Jill agreed to drive to Fort Myers the day before Ralph and he boarded the train. Since Ralph and he were leaving early the following morning, he planned to spend the night with Ralph. Bobby would take them to the station.

The drive to Fort Myers was quicker than either expected, and before they knew it, they were pulling in Ralph's driveway. Reminiscing and discussing their hopes for the future, seemed to have shortened the distance.

"You aren't in a hurry to get home, are you?" Carl asked.

"No. Not at all."

"Good…. I don't see Ralph's car; he's probably spending his last day home with his girlfriend. I'll take my suitcase in and be right back."

"Where're we going?" Jill asked when he returned.

"To the City Yacht Basin."

"Any particular reason?"

"No. Not really. I just feel a little tense about leaving, and walking on the docks, looking at the boats, has always relaxed me."

They walked to the end of the longest dock—his special place. Jill was dressed in jeans, so he suggested they sit on the edge and let their feet dangle. During the summer there were always several boats on the river. This day was no exception.

Jill slid closer to him. "What's the name of this river?"

"She's the Caloosahatchee.... Ralph and I have enjoyed many days on this river. It's more than a mile wide, and I can't count the times we rowed the 12' skiff we built to our campsite on the other side. We didn't explore upriver much, but we did row to the Gulf a few times. There were times when the river would be too rough for a boat as small as ours," with his head and eyes, he motioned to the bridge, "so, to get to our camp, we rode our bikes across The Edison Bridge."

She looked toward the bridge. "The Edison Bridge.... Is the bridge named after the famous inventor, Thomas Edison?"

"Yes."

"I'm sorry that we never got to visit his laboratory and home like you wanted."

"It's one of my favorite places," he moved his eyes from the river to hers, "and I had hoped to share it with you."

"Maybe some day."

He quickly shifted his eyes back to the river. "Not only was Fort Myers Mr. Edison's winter home, it was his friends', Henry Ford and Harvey Firestone's. He also had many famous people visit him, like Charles Lindbergh, President Hoover, John Burroughs, the great naturalist, and many others.

"One day Ford, Firestone, Edison, and Burroughs, who had a long, white beard, were riding around in one of Ford's cars. Ford got out to talk with the filling station attendant when he stopped for gas. When the man finished pumping the gas, Ford said, 'I have a headlight out. Do you have a bulb?' 'Sure do,' the man answered. While the man changed the bulb, Ford said, 'That's Mr. Edison in the front seat, the inventor of the light bulb.' 'You don't say?' 'Yep.' He pointed to the name on the car, 'And I'm

Henry Ford.' Then he asked the man to check the pressure in his tires. 'I see you have some excellent Firestone tires,' the man said. 'Oh, yes,' Ford said, 'nothing but the best. And that's Mr. Firestone sitting in the back seat' 'How 'bout that,' the man said. While checking one of the tires, the man looked up and saw that Mr. Burroughs had his head and beard out the window watching him. 'And, I guess you're going to tell me you're Santa Claus!'"

Jill laughed, then bumped his shoulder with hers. "That didn't really happen."

"I doubt it, but I've heard it told many times, and by different people."

Without looking, Carl sensed that Jill's expression had changed from cheery to serious, and when he looked down and saw her hand moving closer to his, he turned his over to accept it.

As their fingers wove together, she said, "You come here often, don't you?"

"I used to, when something was bothering me."

"Is something bothering you now?"

"Not really."

"Yes, there is…. You don't think I should marry John, do you?"

"I would prefer you didn't, but it's probably because I think no one is good enough for you. He's getting a wonderful girl and, yes,…I'm jealous."

"Are you jealous because I'm getting married, or is it because we're not getting married?"

The answer he wanted to give was on the tip of his tongue, but, instead, he chose to be evasive, "I wish I was getting married."

She smiled, pulled his hand to her lips, kissed it, and said, "Let's go to the Snack House one last time."

When Carl pulled *Blue* against the curb in front of Ralph's house, Jill slid next to him and kissed his cheek. "Don't worry," she said, "Tom and I will take good care of *Blue*."

He stood with both hands on the bottom of the open window and watched Jill adjust the seat and rearview mirror.

When she was satisfied with the seat and mirror, she slowly turned her face to his.

By the sad look in her eyes, and her forced smile, he had an idea what she was going to ask him.

"Were you serious when you said you wished you were getting married?"

"Yes. And I wish it was to you." He knew better than to say what he did, but the words were out, and he didn't regret saying them. He moved to kiss her, but she looked away.

She turned on the ignition, but before starting the engine, and without looking at him, she said, "I love you, Carl."

He leaned in the window, and when she turned to look at him, he said, "I love you, and I always will," then kissed her partially open, quivering lips.

She quickly turned her face from his, and with her head pressed against the top of the steering wheel, she started *Blue's* engine. Then, after shifting into low, she looked back to Carl.

He was overcome with grief when he saw the tears streaming down her cheeks. Her lips looked swollen, and her chin was trembling as she tried to keep from crying, but when she let out *Blue's* clutch and started to move, she lost control of her emotions and began sobbing loudly. He knew it would be a long time, if ever, before the memory of hearing her crying as she drove away would fade.

The urge to run after her, waving his arms, trying to get her to stop, was overwhelming, but it was too late. *I had my chance.*

He watched until she turned the corner and out of sight.

* * * *

Boot Camp was difficult. The days were long and the training was hard, which left little time for writing. Ralph managed to get a few letters off to his mother and girlfriend, and Carl wrote a few addressed to Tom, Joyce and Jill; he had a little to say to each. He wanted to write a separate letter to Jill, but was afraid of what he might say.

Even though the days were long, the nine weeks passed quickly. Ralph and Carl's test scores were high, so they were able to get their first choice of class. Ralph chose electrician and Carl chose diesel mechanic. He figured being a diesel mechanic would help with his chosen profession—a charter boat captain.

It was early on a Tuesday morning when the train arrived; Bobby was there to pick them up. After a hearty breakfast, prepared by Ralph's mother, Ralph and his girlfriend drove Carl to Naples.

"God, it's good to see you!" Jill said as they embraced. "I was about to think you weren't going to make it in time for my wedding."

"You know I wouldn't miss seeing you get hitched. I wasn't sure when I would arrive, and since Ralph volunteered to drive me here, I thought I'd surprise you."

"Well, you did. I was beginning to think I'd have to reschedule."

"It's this Saturday. Right?"

"Yep. Four more days."

Carl came close to saying "it's not too late to change your mind," but instead he chose to ask, "Are you getting excited."

"Yes. But more nervous than excited. What was supposed to be a small wedding, with only our families and a few friends, has become humongous. As you know, his father is going to marry us in his church, and I think the whole congregation will be there."

"Wow! I'd be nervous too…. Oh! I'm sorry," he said when he realized he had forgotten to introduce Ralph's girlfriend. "Frances, I'd like you to meet Jill. Jill, this is Frances."

They embraced and told each other how pleased they were to meet, then Jill embraced Ralph. "Did you get my invitation?"

"I got it, and we'll be here."

"Where's Tom and your mother?" Carl asked.

"Tom's out on his boat, he had a charter, and Mom's doing some more shopping."

Ralph said they couldn't stay long; he and Frances had to be getting back to Fort Myers.

Jill was standing next to Carl as they watched Ralph and Frances drive away. The touch of her hand on his back was all the encouragement he needed to put his arm around her and caress her close to his side. With their arms around each other, they continued to look in the direction of Ralph's car, even when they could no longer see it.

"Carl…"

"Yes?"

"Tell me I'm doing the right thing."

"You aren't having doubts, are you?"

"Some." She sat on the couch and patted the cushion beside her, encouraging him to sit. "He lied to me the other day. It wasn't even about something he needed to lie about. If he chooses to be dishonest about something trivial, what will he do or say if he does something really bad?…He promised he would never lie again. I want to believe him, but I wonder. And…I can't get over what you said when *Blue* and I drove away."

He knew what he said, but was reluctant to say it. "Have a safe trip?"

"No…. You know what you said."

He felt her hand grasp his a little tighter. "That I wish I was marrying you and I love you?"

"Yes."

"I do love you, and I always will. And, I feel you love me. But, we had our chance and I, or we, blew it. Now, you have a wedding planned, and, more than anything, I want you to be happy. So, go for it." That was not what he wanted to say, but he didn't want to confuse her.

"I love John and I feel certain he loves me. The few problems we've had are minor, so maybe I'm expecting too much. Surely his father's influence will contribute to him being a good husband and father."

He hoped she was right, but had his doubts.

To take his mind off Jill's upcoming wedding, Carl kept himself busy by helping Tom with his charters. He also called Vicky, a girl he had dated several times. They made plans to date after Jill's wedding.

Vicky was one of the few girls that had enjoyed Carl, and the pleasure of *Blue's* back seat, without expecting any kind of commitment. Being with her after Jill's wedding was something he looked forward to, but even though his craving was strong, he could not bring himself to be with her before the wedding.

Carl felt John wasn't comfortable with him living in the same house with Jill, but when Jill told him that John did not trust them, he was furious. "Doesn't he trust you?"

"I think he does, but he's curious about what may have happened while we lived together for almost two years."

"It's difficult for me to believe that anyone who knows you could have those thoughts. Especially, your future husband! What an idiot!...I'm sorry. I didn't mean to call him an idiot."

"Yes you did. And I understand why. But, let's not let you thinking he's an idiot affect our friendship."

"I won't. I promise.... But, so he'll feel comfortable, I'll avoid being alone with you. That should help."

"Thanks for understanding. There's nothing I want more than for you and John to be friends."

"I want that too." *I have no desire to be his friend, but, if being friends will help her feel comfortable when we're together, I'll do my best.*

Experiencing a wedding was something Carl had never done, but if Jill and John's was an example of a beautiful wedding, theirs had to be one of the most beautiful.

All eyes were on Jill as she held Tom's arm while walking down the aisle. To Carl, the display of happiness her eyes and smile expressed was electrifying, even more when her eyes searched him out, then fixed on his. He returned her smile and gave a little nod. Without being obvious, but enough for him to see, she dipped her head before shifting her eyes from his. Tom also looked at Carl, but his smile was somewhat reserved.

Where Jill and John went on their honeymoon was kept secret; only Joyce and Tom knew. When they returned, they would live in the apartment that joined the church parsonage. Unfortunately, for Carl, they wouldn't return before he had to leave.

Chapter 10

▼

It was twelve weeks before Carl got another leave. Again, he and Ralph finished at the top of their classes, which allowed them to get their first choice of available ships. The aircraft carrier *Forrestal* was scheduled to go on a world cruise, so they chose her. At the time, the *Forrestal* was in port, having some routine maintenance, which gave them the opportunity to take a two-week leave.

Bobby was waiting for them at the train station; this time Ralph's girlfriend was with him. Carl had mentioned to Ralph that he was anxious to get to Naples. Jill's letters had hinted that her marriage was not going well, and he wanted to know why. Ralph's mother wasn't home; she had to go in to work early. So, after skipping breakfast, Ralph and Frances drove him to Naples. They were in a hurry, so as soon as they arrived, they headed back to Fort Myers.

"Oh, Carl," Joyce said while they embraced, "I'm so glad you're here. How have you been?"

"Great! I love the Navy." He noticed her eyes were red and her smile seemed reserved; her face lacked its normal glow. "How have you been?"

"Couldn't be better."

He pulled away from her a little and looked into her eyes. "You're not being honest with me…. What's wrong?"

"It's Jill." She returned to his arms and pressed her face against his chest. "John's a jerk! And I'm stupid for encouraging Jill to marry him. Tom tried to warn me, but I wouldn't listen. Like Jill, I was captivated by his religious background and fake charm. Jill knows she made a big mistake by marrying the lying bastard, but there's not much she can do about it."

"What's he done to cause you this much grief?"

"He's seeing another girl."

"What!" he shouted, then pulled out a chair from the table for her and another for him.

"In the three months they've been married, he's had three jobs; the first two only lasted about a week. His father and the church have been supporting them. This last job is in Fort Myers. He delivers bread. And occasionally, so he says, he has to stay in Fort Myers overnight.

"He told Jill he was staying with one of the guys he works with. Jill believed him until last week. That's when she got a call from one of her girlfriends who moved to Fort Myers. The friend works in a florist shop, and when she asked Jill if she knew a girl named Lynette Taylor, and Jill said she didn't, the friend said John had sent her flowers."

"I went to school with Lynette. I can't believe she'd go with a married man…. What did John say when Jill asked him about her?"

"He said the fellow he's staying with is dating Lynette, and when the fellow asked him to order some flowers for her, the person taking the order must've thought they were from him."

"Does Jill believe him?"

"Not at all. She's suspected he's been cheating ever since they returned from their honeymoon. This just confirms her suspicions."

"She needs to get out of that mess."

"I agree. But it won't be as easy as you might think."

He put his face in his hands. "She's pregnant."

"Yes. At least two months."

"What's she going to do?"

"She wants to move back home, and Tom and I think she should, but she's afraid that John and his influential father will make her appear to be a tramp and blame her for their separation, which will make getting a divorce more difficult. Tom wants to confront John and his father, but Jill wants him to wait until she has proof."

"Maybe I can help. I'll go talk with her."

Even before *Blue* came to a stop, Carl saw Jill coming to greet him. They rushed to each other's open arms, and as they embraced he felt her tears against his cheek. With her head on his shoulder and his arm around her, they silently walked to her apartment. She had barely begun to tell him that marrying John was a mistake, when the door flew open and John's father walked in.

His eyes were filled with anger. "What are you doing here!" he shouted while walking toward Carl.

"Hi, I'm Carl. I came to see Jill."

He ignored Carl's extended hand. "I know who you are. Don't you think it would be more discreet to come visit when my son is home?"

"I understand he's not home too often."

"So, you knew he's working and wouldn't be home."

"What in the hell are you insinuating!" Jill asked.

"You know how bad this looks! My son's out trying to make an honest living while you're entertaining an old boyfriend."

"Carl is a friend. Not, as you say, 'an old boyfriend.'"

"It doesn't matter what he is. I want him out of here. I don't want my congregation to have more to talk about than they already do."

"I assume," Carl butted in, "you're referring to your son."

"Not my son! You idiot! My son's wife!"

Carl couldn't believe what this, supposedly, man of the cloth had said. He stared at him for a moment, then picked up the phone.

"Hello, Joyce.... I need for you to do me and Jill a big, big favor.... Come get her out of this house and away from John's 'asshole' father."

"You better watch your mouth!"

Carl glanced from the phone, then back to it. "You're coming right over?...Good. I'll wait for you." After hanging up, he held his hand on the phone for a few seconds, then walked to the door and opened it. "You can leave now. Your nosy members have seen you here and know Jill's safe." His anger began to build when he noticed John's father was not moving. He continued to hold the door open with one hand and motioned with the other. "Get out!" he shouted.

John's father cautiously made his way past Carl. "I'll be back." He had to have the last word, and Carl let him.

"My, God!" Carl said. "What kind of pastor, or minister, or whatever he calls himself, is he?"

"He claims to be an Ordained Minister, but I have my doubts."

"Can I help you pack?"

Jill couldn't answer; she could only nod.

"By the way John's father acted, I think John has convinced him that you're the one cheating."

"Mom told you?"

"Yes."

They were putting Jill's belongings in suitcases, paper bags, boxes, and even pillowcases when Joyce arrived. Jill wrapped her arms around her mother and began to cry. Between her sobs she managed to say, "I'm coming home, Mom."

"Good," was all her mother could say.

They loaded what they could in Joyce's car.

"We can come back tonight and get the rest," Joyce said.

"No," Carl said. "Please don't come back tonight. If you come back, you'll bring Tom, and if John's father talks to Tom like he did me, he'll be facing his congregation tomorrow with two black eyes and a few missing teeth, if he can face them at all. I'd come back with you, but Ralph and I have some plans. And, unless you need me to help you unload the car, I should be getting on the road."

"We can get it," Joyce said.

"Will you be coming home tonight?" Jill asked.

"Probably. But if not, I'll be back in the morning."

"Carl Sanford! What a pleasant surprise," Lynette's mother said. "Please tell me you came to inquire about Lynette. I always wanted you guys to fall in love and marry."

"Really?"

"You know I did. It's not too late. She's still available."

"Is she here?"

"Oh, no. She moved in with one of the girls she works with; she's an operator for the phone company. Would you like to have her address and phone number?"

"Yes, if you don't think she'll mind."

"She won't mind a bit. Let me get something to write on.... I won't call her. I want her to be surprised."

Carl thanked her, and she wished him a merry Christmas.

He couldn't get over how pleased he was when he had realized he would be home for Christmas—now it was the farthest thing from his mind.

Instead of calling Lynette, he decided to surprise her, but first, he stopped by Ralph's and borrowed his car. If John was planning to visit Lynette, he didn't want him to be tipped off by seeing *Blue* parked in front of her house.

"Hi. I'm Carl Sanford," he said to the attractive girl who answered the door. "Is Lynette in?"

"Hi, Carl," she said, then opened the door wider, inviting him in. "She's in the shower, getting ready to go out. Have a seat. I'll tell her you're here."

He was barely seated when the girl returned. "Lynette said she'll be right out.... I'm Sara."

He quickly stood and grasped her hand. "Nice meeting you, Sara."

"You don't know me, but I know a lot about you."

"How do you know about me?" he asked.

"Lynette and her mother are always talking about you. Her mother can't believe Lynette let you get away. And, now that I've met you, I understand why."

"Thanks." He didn't know what else to say.

"I heard you're in the Navy. Are you home on leave?"

"Yes. A two-week-leave."

"Only two weeks and you're not with your girlfriend?"

"Not tonight." She had made it clear that she was attracted to him, and any other night, he would've asked similar questions.

"Well! It really is Carl Sanford!" Lynette said when she entered the room. "And looking better than ever."

"So are you." He stood to accept her outstretched, beckoning arms. He had forgotten how beautiful she was, even without makeup. She was dressed only in a robe. Her shiny, black hair, still wet from her shower, felt cold against his cheek. To savor the aroma of the fresh, clean smell of her fragrant shampoo, he pressed his face in her wet hair and breathed in deeply. "God, you smell good!"

"Thanks." They slowly relaxed their arms, but she left hers on his shoulders and his were around her waist. "What brings you to see me?"

He realized she was confused. It was not like him to visit someone unannounced. They had dated a few times while in high school, but were never close. She preferred an active social life: school dances, being with her friends, parties, and anything else that kept her on the go. Because of her good looks and charm, he had tried to adapt, but it didn't take him long to realize her lifestyle was more than he could afford. Especially, while making payments on his mother's big Buick. He stopped asking her out, but they remained good friends.

"I'm concerned about something, and I'd like to discuss it with you," he said.

While holding her robe together, she sat in the middle of the couch. He sat beside her.

"What's your problem?" she asked.

He would've preferred to talk in private, but when he looked toward Sara, sitting in a chair opposite them, she didn't take the hint. "I'm very uncomfortable asking you this, but it's important that I know."

"This sounds serious."

"It is.... Are you dating a fellow named John?"

"Yes, I am."

"Does he work for a bread company and lives in Naples?"

"Yes. Has something happened to him?"

"Not yet."

"What do you mean, 'not yet?'"

"Are you aware that his wife is pregnant?"

"He's married!" Sara screamed.

Lynette covered her mouth with her hands. Her eyes filled with tears, but she didn't remove her hands.

"How do you know this?" Sara asked.

"He's married to my uncle's daughter, the one I've been living with."

Lynette lowered her hands. "No, Carl, I didn't know." She pressed her face against his chest and began to cry.

Trying to comfort her, he put his arms around her and held her close. Sara joined them on the couch and also embraced her. After a minute or so, Sara stood and began pacing the floor. "That son of a bitch," she said, a little louder than a whisper.... "That son of a bitch!"

There was an almost silent knock on the door; Carl didn't hear it; Lynette's crying muffled the sound. Sara was moving toward the door when it opened.

"Whose car is parked in front?" John asked. He was taking his jacket off when he noticed Carl and Lynette on the couch. "What're you doing here?"

Before Carl could answer, Sara slapped John across the face. The slap was loud; Carl knew she had used all her strength.

"You bastard!" she screamed. "Why do you think he's here?"

John drew back to return her slap when, out of the corner of his eye, he saw Carl stand.

"What kind of lies have you been telling them?" he asked.

"Carl wouldn't lie!" Lynette shouted. "Now get out, and I never want to see you again!" When he didn't move, she shouted even louder, "Get out!"

Carl walked past him and opened the door. "You heard her. Now, get out." John mumbled something when he went out the door.

"What did you say?" Carl asked.

"I said I'll take care of you later."

"I can hardly wait."

When Carl returned to Lynette, she was lying on her back with a pillow covering her face. Sara was sitting beside her.

"I'm sorry that I'm the one who exposed him," Carl said, "but I just knew you would never date a married man."

"I realize it took a lot for you to tell me, and I want you to know that I appreciate finding out before I broke up a marriage."

"It's not your fault. But his marriage is over, and he's lost a wonderful girl. He's an idiot."

"Yes, he's an idiot, and I'm an idiot for believing him and falling in love.... So much for a merry Christmas."

"We'll have a merry Christmas," Sara said. "Now you can rejoice for getting out of a relationship before getting hurt more than you are."

Lynette removed the pillow from her face and looked up at Carl. "You may think I don't, but I do appreciate you telling me.... There's one person that's going to be pleased."

"Who?" Carl asked.

"Her mother," Sara said before Lynette could answer.

"Mom never liked him."

"But we know who she does like. Don't we?" Sara said.

"We tried," Lynette said. "God knows we tried. Didn't we?"

"Yes we did.... We may not have fallen in love, but we sure became good friends."

Sara looked back at Lynette. "If you and Carl are just good friends, can I have him?"

They all laughed. It was good to see Lynette smile and hear her laugh. Carl figured it was a good time to leave. "I better get going. I have to get Ralph's car back to him."

"Where's your car?" Lynette asked. "I heard you made it into a real beauty."

"It's at Ralph's. I didn't want John to see it and know I was here. He wouldn't have come in if he had seen my car, and I wanted to see his face when he discovered me here.... I'll call in a few days, just to make sure he's not harassing you."

"Thanks."

Sara stood and extended her arms. "Yes. Please call."

They embraced, then he bent down to Lynette and kissed her on the cheek. "Good luck."

Carl was surprised to see John's car. He assumed John was waiting to ask him to not tell Jill. When he saw that John was not in his car, he became suspicious. At about the same time he turned toward Ralph's car, he heard Sara scream, "Watch out behind you!"

His reflexes caused him to duck, and John's fist grazed the right side of his head. He surprised John by hitting him with his left—his father had taught him to lead with his left. By the sound and feel, he knew he had done some severe damage to John's face. As John fell back, Carl pursued him, then hit him with his right, knocking him back even farther and to the ground.

The anger and rage Carl felt was more than he had ever experienced, and he was anxious for John to stand. For protection, John stood with his arms and hands in front of his face. Carl found himself dancing around his opponent as if he were in the ring, waiting for the opportune moment. With his right, Carl hit him hard in the stomach, and when John buckled toward him, he stepped to his right and hit him in the face with his left, knocking him to the ground. Carl stood above him, watching him squirm and listening to his moans.

"Have you had enough, or would you like me to beat on you some more?"

John shook his head and with great difficulty said, "Enough."

When Carl became aware of his surroundings, he saw Sara standing before him. They made eye contact and she rushed to embrace him. "Are you all right?" she asked.

"I'm fine. But I think I hurt John really bad."

"He deserves to be hurt. Sneaking up on you from behind and trying to hit you with something."

"What do you mean, 'hit me with something?'"

"He had an object in his hand. I don't know what it was, but I saw it when he drew back to hit you."

"I thought he swung at me with his fist."

"Here it is," she said.

"That son of a bitch!" Carl said when she handed it to him. "He tried to hit me with a blackjack! He must've dropped it when I hit him. What a no-account bastard. Damn! I'm glad you called out to me."

"And I'm glad you ducked." She took his hand in hers. "You're bleeding."

He was not aware of the blood dripping from his left hand, or the pain. "I guess I am." He grimaced with pain when she straightened his fingers.

"Let's go in and wash your hand and put some medicine on it…. I'll call the guy John stays with and ask him to come get him." She looked down at John, still curled up on the ground. "I don't think he's going anywhere, do you?"

"I don't think he can."

"What happened to your hand?" Lynette asked. She had been in the bathroom during the fight.

"As he was leaving," Sara said, "John tried to hit him with this." She held the blackjack up for Lynette to see. "But, Carl beat the hell out of him."

"Oh, no! How bad is he? And, where is he."

"He's not hurt bad, and he's outside," Sara said. She knew how gullible Lynette was, and if she was aware of his condition, she would bring him in, wash and doctor his wounds, and he would be right back in her arms. "Here…you wash Carl's hand while I call his roommate to come get him."

"He can't drive? I'll drive him home."

"Oh, no you won't!" Carl said. "I want you to promise me that you'll stop talking to him on the phone and never see him again. He's a lying, sneaky bastard, and I don't want to see you hurt. Look at that!" He pointed to the blackjack on the counter where Sara had laid it. "That could've killed me!…Instead of Sara calling his roommate, she should be calling the police. So, please Lynette. Please don't go out to him. And promise me you'll not get involved with him again."

"I promise. Now, let's wash your hand."

By the way his knuckles looked and felt he knew he had hit John in the mouth and probably knocked out a few teeth, or at least loosened some.

When Sara finished making the call, Carl saw her look out the door.

"What's he doing?" he asked.

"He's sitting up…. He'll be all right." She didn't want Lynette to worry. "His roommate said he'll be right over. The roommate's girlfriend will drive John's car home."

"Good," Carl said. "I was wondering what to do with his car. I sure as hell didn't want him to come back after it."

"There you go," Lynette said when she finished bandaging his hand, "good as new."

Carl picked up the blackjack, evaluated it for a moment, then put it in his pocket. He looked at Sara and smiled. "Thanks."

"That didn't take long," Sara said when she saw car lights reflecting on the front window.

By the time Carl arrived outside, John's roommate had John loaded in his car.

"What happened to John?" his roommate asked.

"I beat the hell out of him."

"I can see that, but why."

"He's married to…"

"He's married!"

"Yes. To my best friend. She's pregnant, and the bastard's cheating on her."

"That son of a bitch! He told me he had a girlfriend in Naples, and I figured he was cheating on Lynette. I thought that was bad, but this is too much. As soon as he can see to drive, he's out of my house."

"Well, he sure as hell won't have a wife to go back to."

"I better be getting him home and put some ice on his face. I don't want him staying with me any longer than he has to."

"You might want to take him to the emergency room and get his ribs checked."

Chapter 11

By the time Carl pulled into Ralph's driveway, his hand was beginning to throb.

"What did you do to your hand?" Ralph asked.

"I got in a fight with Jill's husband."

"Did you do good?"

"I did great.... Do you mind if I make a couple calls to Naples? I'll reimburse you."

"Sure. But you can't pay for them."

Joyce answered. "How's Jill?" he asked.

"She's fine, a little upset, but getting better. Where are you?"

"In Fort Myers."

"I figured you'd go looking for John. Did you find him?"

"Yes."

"Is he in the hospital?"

"No, but he probably should be."

"Good."

"Is Jill awake?"

"She's sleeping. Do you want me to wake her?"

"No. I just need the number of her asshole father-in-law. I'd like to let him know where he can find his sorry son. Do you have it?"

"Yes," Joyce chuckled, "I have the asshole's number. The number to his residence is unlisted, but I have it. Can you imagine a Minister with an unlisted number?" Before he could answer, she gave him the number. "Will you be coming home tonight?"

"Yes, but don't wait up for me."

"Oh, no. Tom and I would never do that."

He laughed. "I'll see you in an hour or so."

"Who is this?" was the way John's father answered the phone.

"Carl. Your daughter-in-law's…"

"I know who you are. What do you want at this time of night?"

"I just thought you'd like to know that your sorry son will be coming home soon."

"Don't call my son 'sorry.'"

"What would you call an adulterer, a liar, and someone who tried to kill me?"

"You're trying to cause trouble and making this up. John would never do any of those things. I'm not listening to any more."

Carl tried to call back, but all he got was a busy signal.

Like he thought, Joyce and Tom were waiting for him. They were anxious to hear what happened and wanted to know every detail. When Carl finished, Joyce asked what John's father had to say.

"He wouldn't listen to anything I said. He hung up on me."

"He hung up on you!" Tom said, while putting on his shoes. "What do you say we go over and have a little midnight prayer session with that controlling bastard?"

Tom didn't bother ringing the doorbell. He beat on the door with the side of his fist; it sounded to Carl like he was going to break it down.

From inside the house, they heard, "Who is it?"

"Tom and Carl," Tom answered, "We want to talk with you."

"I have no desire to listen to either of you. And, if you don't go away, I'll call the police."

"That's a damn good idea. Call the police. We'll wait here until they arrive."

"I won't come out until you agree to clean up your vocabulary."

"Can you believe he wants to control me?" Tom said to Carl. He turned back to the door and yelled, "I'm not going to agree to anything! You pompous bastard! So, open this damn door and come out or call the police!"

The door slowly opened. "Hurry up and start talking. I have a sermon to give in the morning, and I need my rest."

"I doubt if you'll get much rest after you hear what Carl has to say."

"I'm not listening to any more of his lies."

John's father was standing behind the half-open door, and when it began to close, Tom kicked it in, knocking the minister back to the middle of the room.

Tom was shaking so much his voice was trembling. "Get your hypocritic ass out here and listen to Carl or I'll come in there and drag you out!"

He joined them, but left his door open. "I'll have you know, I'm not a hypocrite and you have no right to call me one."

"Oh," Tom said. "You think no one knows about your affair?"

The minister quickly reached for the door and closed it behind him. "All right, Carl, what do you have to say?"

"I discovered that John is, or was, seeing a girl in Fort Myers. She had no idea he was married."

"I don't believe you. John wouldn't do that."

"Her name is Lynette Taylor. I'll give you her phone number if you'd like to call and confirm it. I'll even give you her mother's phone number. They both have been deceived and are very upset. And, if you're interested in the truth, and don't believe me, I suggest you call."

"I'll ask John when he visits tomorrow, or," he looked back at one of his many clocks, "today now. He never misses church."

"He'll miss this one."

"Why do you say that?"

"Because I beat the hell out of him."

"You beat my son?" The minister snickered, as if there was no way Carl would have a chance in a fight with his son.

"You can judge for yourself when you see him. He's probably going to have some wild-ass story to tell you; like he was hit by a truck, or he was trying to keep an old lady from getting robbed by a gang of boys and they beat him, or something similar."

"That's a good one," Tom said.

"I don't think your accusations are funny!"

"Well," Tom said, while holding his open hand toward Carl, "let me show you something that's not a damn bit funny."

Carl reached in his pocket, pulled out the blackjack, and gave it to Tom.

"Do you recognize this?" Tom asked.

"Not really."

"By your answer, I think you do." He glared at the minister a moment before continuing. "Your wonderful son tried to hit Carl with this, and he would've if someone hadn't warned Carl."

"That's not true! John would never do that!"

"I have two witnesses," Carl said.

"Two of your friends?"

"No," Carl answered. "One is. The other, I met tonight."

"The truth is," Tom said while pointing his finger in the minister's face, "even though you have no desire to hear the truth, your son could've killed Carl. Another truth is, he's cheating on his pregnant wife, which can be verified by the girl he was seeing, her mother, the girl's roommate, and John's roommate and his girlfriend. These are facts I will be more than pleased to spread through the community if..."

"If, what?"

"If John doesn't stay away from my daughter. I also expect him to agree to a quick divorce, and I expect him, or you, to pay the doctor and hospital for the delivery of her baby..."

"Don't you mean, their baby?" the minister asked.

"No. I meant what I said, her baby. Jill wants full custody. She doesn't want alimony or child support, and John is to have no visitation rights. If you or John don't agree with what I've said, we'll expect alimony and child support, and I'll destroy your reputation in your church and this community. And, if you leave, I'll find you."

"I'll have to ask John about this."

"Why do you have to ask John? You know you'll be the one footing the bill. You also know how tough Judge Stanley is on cheating fathers. And, not that it matters, but Judge Stanley and I are close friends. We'll give you and John until the end of the week to make up your minds. That should be long enough."

"I'll think about it."

"You do that.... From what Carl tells me, you should also be thinking about getting your son to a doctor...and a dentist." Tom paused for a moment. "So, I can expect an answer in a few days?"

"By the end of the week."

They were on their way home when Carl asked, "How did you know he was having an affair?"

"I didn't. But I think I hit a nerve. Don't you?"

"Yes, I do. As they say: 'Like father. Like son.'"

"That's what I was thinking."

Early the next morning, Tom, Jill, and Carl picked up the rest of Jill's stuff; they figured John had not healed enough to drive. After lunch, Carl and Jill went to town and bought his mother a Christmas card. It was difficult to find a store open on Sunday, but they did.

To give Lynette some time to gain control of her emotions, Carl waited until later in the afternoon to call. Sara answered the phone.

"How are you girls doing?"

"I'm doing fine, but Lynette's having a problem dealing with the guilt she feels. She wants to call John's wife and apologize."

"I've told Jill that Lynette would never go with a married man and, just like her, Lynette was conned. I also mentioned that I think it would be best if they never meet or talk. That way, Jill won't have a face or voice to identify with John's cheating, and Lynette won't know who she, unintentionally, hurt. Communicating with each other will only slow their efforts to forget John and get on with their lives. Do you think I'm right?"

"Yes, I do, and I'll let Lynette know how we feel when she returns."

"She's not there?"

"No. She's helping her mother prepare for Christmas.... What are you doing for Christmas?"

"I'm going to spend it with my uncle and his family. What are your plans?"

"Lynette's mother has invited me to have Christmas with them.... Will you be coming to Fort Myers after Christmas?"

"I hadn't planned to."

"Will you? I'd like to see you."

"Let's see," Carl thought for a moment, "Christmas is Tuesday, so how about Wednesday?"

"Looking forward to it."

"Me, too."

* * * *

There was much concern about how Jill would deal with her emotions, but there was no indication that she even thought about John or her predicament, which pleased everyone. It was obvious to all that she was glad to be home, and by Christmas day she had returned to being her jovial self. It was as if she had never married.

The only contact Carl had with his mother was when he phoned her to wish her a merry Christmas. She thanked him, and that's about all that was said. They didn't talk long enough for him to know whether she was drinking or not. She seemed anxious to get off the phone.

* * * *

Even before the door closed, Carl was surprised with an aggressive embrace and kiss.

"God! I've looked forward to this day," Sara said.

"Me, too."

He pulled away a little to check out her face and eyes; both were caked with makeup.

They agreed on a movie.

After the movie, and a burger at Buck's Restaurant, they returned to her home. While sitting on the couch, petting and talking, he learned she was from Connecticut, and when he said he had always wanted to visit her home state, she described it until he wished he had not expressed an interest in visiting it.

She only stopped talking when he said it was getting late and he had to go. He started to stand, but she held him back, laid her body on his, and began kissing him passionately. She positioned her large breasts against his chest and moved them up and down, and back and forth. She kissed his neck, his ears, and his lips. Her assertive tongue found his, but only for a moment. She licked his neck, his ears, and eyes before returning to his mouth.

He was uncomfortable and felt her exaggerated show of passion was not sincere. It was orchestrated to impress, and was turning him off instead of on.

"I'm sorry," he said. "It's getting late, and I better be going."

She pulled away. He sensed she knew she had come on too strong. He stood, and while putting his shirt back in his pants, he looked at her lying on the couch. She looked rejected and confused.

"Will you come back tomorrow?…I promise I won't molest you."

He leaned over her and kissed her gently on the lips. "Promise?"

"I promise."

While kissing her, he struggled to lift her sweater. To help him, she arched her back. She was braless. He caressed one of her beautiful breasts in his hand and kissed its excited nipple. "Tomorrow."

"Tomorrow."

He wondered why he had agreed to return.

Carl was stunned by Sara's appearance. It was drastically different from the night before: her hair was pulled back in more of a casual style, not pouffy; her eye shadow was light, just enough to highlight her sexy eyes, not dark and gaudy; her beautiful face was not hidden with gobs of unnecessary makeup; her lips had just enough color to look natural, not the exaggerated, bright red that, after kissing her, he had asked her to wipe some off, and her sweater was casual and not as revealing. She looked like she did the first night they met.

While they embraced, the aroma of her scented soap, still fresh from her shower, and the delicate smell of her perfume that was perfect for her, created a yearning to tighten his arms around her and press her firm breasts against his chest. And he did.

With his face nestled against her neck he savored the clean fragrance coming from her hair and body. He parted his lips to taste her inviting neck, then slowly eased his partially open mouth to her anxious lips.

He was pleased to find her lips parted only a little. It was a delicate kiss. Not like the ones he had been uncomfortable with the night before, where she opened her mouth to the maximum and tried to get as much of his face in as possible. Instead of her tongue thrashing around in his mouth, she eased it in. He savored her soft, moist lips and enjoyed the sweet smell of her tantalizing breath without the strong taste of lipstick.

"Wow!" he whispered in her ear. "Which person is the real you? This one, or the one last night?"

"This one…. I misread you. I thought you would like an aggressive girl, and that's what I tried to be; I even dressed the part."

Since he was aware that Lynette enjoyed playing jokes on her friends, he thought she might have told Sara to be aggressive. "Did Lynette mislead you?"

"No. I misled myself. I was impressed by how tough and independent you were the other night and thought you'd like a girl that was the same. I guess I tried too hard. When I became aware that my actions were making you uncomfortable, I felt cheap. I thought, when you left, you'd never come back, and I wouldn't have blamed you if you didn't, but I'm glad you did."

"Me, too."

They were in a tight embrace and kissing when, from behind him, he heard Lynette say, "Well!...I see you've experienced his kisses. Aren't they the best?"

"The very best."

"That, Carl Sanford, is the one thing about you I remember the most. You were always one helluva kisser. I wish we had experienced sex."

"What!" Sara shouted. "You mean..."

"Never. Not once."

"Actually," Sara said as she held his arm and directed him to the door, "I'm glad to know you didn't."

They went to a drive-in theater, but didn't see much of the movie. Except for Eve, he had not been with a girl who enjoyed sex as much as Sara, and he had been with several. He and *Blue* had quite a reputation, especially *Blue's* back seat. He had heard some refer to it as the "Sacrificial Altar."

Being aware that he had the Navy to finish, and she had college, allowed them to relax and enjoy each other without the pressure of commitment. And they did.

Before leaving to visit Sara, Carl's mornings and early afternoons were spent talking and doing things with Jill. When he left to visit Sara, Jill would always tell him to have fun. He always answered, "I'll try." They never discussed who he was going to visit.

Jill had adapted to being back home much better than Carl expected. Her little belly was the only indication that she had married and left home. John was never brought up in their conversations.

Carl found it interesting that, while driving home after being with Sara, his thoughts were not about her. They were about Jill. The trip to and from Fort Myers wasn't the same without Jill.

He missed her laughter, her humor, and her enthusiasm when she saw or spoke of something that interested her. He missed how all the waiters at the Snack House recognized her and called her by name, and how she always complimented them on their speed, their accuracy, and how much she enjoyed whatever she ordered.

He missed sitting and sharing his special place on the dock, and when it dawned on him that the Snack House and his special place had become his and Jill's special places, he realized why he had not shared them with Sara.

It was Saturday, his last night with Sara. He had told her earlier in the week that since he was scheduled to leave on Tuesday, he was spending Sunday and Monday in Naples. It was their last night together, and they wanted to make the most of it. And they did.

* * * *

It seemed to Carl that he had just closed his eyes when he heard Jill call from the kitchen, "Breakfast is ready!"

He forced himself out of bed. "I'll be right there!" he yelled. "Do I have time for a shower?"

"No."

To save time, he put on the same pants and shirt he wore the night before, and then shuffled to the kitchen.

Jill placed a plate of bacon, eggs, and toast before him.

"Wow!" she said. "I like your girlfriend's perfume. What is it?"

He looked down at his wrinkled shirt. "I…I…"

She smiled and patted him on the shoulder. "I'm kidding." She paused before continuing, "I got some good news yesterday."

"What? John's going to have to wear dentures?"

"Better than that, although I hope he does.… His father called. John wants a divorce and agrees with all my conditions. I gave him the name and number of my attorney and suggested he call for an appointment. The papers should be ready for John's signature sometime after the first of the year. Now, let's go somewhere and celebrate."

"Where do you have in mind?"

"I want to go to Marco. I understand they're dredging canals and building houses. And while it's still uninhabited, I'd like to walk on the beach like we used to. Then, I'd like to have lunch at that great seafood restaurant. The one built on an old barge."

"The Ship Ahoy? The one at the foot of the bridge in Goodland?"

"Yes. That's the one."

"After my grandfather, Captain Jack, sold his schooner, the *Eureka*, to Captain Ferguson Hall, Captain Ferg installed a diesel engine in her and towed that barge from the Keys to Goodland."

"Really?"

"Yes, he did. My grandfather and Captain Ferg used to tell me some wild stories about their experiences aboard the *Eureka*. I didn't appreciate their stories then. I was too young. I sure wish they were around to tell me again."

"We better hurry if we're going to get back in time for you to get to Fort Myers."

"I'm not going to Fort Myers today."

"Why? Is 'whoever' finished with you? Or, are you finished with her?"

"It was a mutual thing. We had nothing in common and knew from the beginning our relationship was only temporary."

"Sort of like when the monkey made love to the skunk: He didn't get all he wanted, but got all he could stand."

He laughed, and said, "You've heard Tom say that saying, haven't you?"

"A few times.... Hurry up. Get your shower and let's go."

As far as they could see, both north and south, they were the only ones on Marco Beach. It was surprisingly warm for the last of December and there was hardly any wind; the Gulf was, as the old timers say: "slick-calm." The tide was out, which left little water inside a sandbar where Carl used to dig for clams. He told Jill to watch for squirts of water.

"I see one!" she shouted. "And there's another."

Carl had seen them too. With Jill right along with him, he rushed to where they saw the squirts. Soon they had that night's dinner; enough for a large chowder with some to fry.

"How are we going to get them home?" Jill asked.

"I have a tarpaulin and a croker sack in *Blue*. I'll run back and get the sack to carry them in. Then I'll spread out the tarp, to keep the salt water from getting in *Blue's* trunk, and put the sack of clams on it. Wait here. I'll be right back." He didn't want her to exert herself.

When the clams were loaded in *Blue*, they returned to the beach and began walking in the opposite direction. The water was not warm enough to be comfortable, so they chose to walk in the sand. Since Carl was taller than Jill, he was on the low side; their hips were about the same height. To stop their hips from bumping, he put his arm around her at the same time she put her arm around him. They pulled each other close and the bumping stopped. A comfort, felt only with Jill, flowed through him. He assumed she felt it too. Neither chose to admit it.

They were silent for quite a while.

"Have you decided on a name for your baby girl?"

"What makes you think it's a girl?"

"I don't know. Maybe it's just wishful thinking."

"I hope it's a girl too. If it is, I'm going to name her 'Tommie.'"

"I like that. Tom will be proud. And if it's a boy?"

"If it's a boy, I'll name him 'Thomas.' I thought about Carlie and Carlos, but…"

"No! No! No!" he said. "Tommie and Thomas are perfect."

"Don't you think it's time for lunch? My stomach is telling me it's ready for a grouper sandwich."

"Mine, too."

They turned around; their embrace was even closer than before. "You're leaving Tuesday?"

"Bright and early."

"Have you made plans on how you're getting there?"

He tightened his arm around her and put his cheek against her hair. "You know I have."

Without asking, she knew she was going to Fort Myers and returning with *Blue*.

Chapter 12

It was Monday, New Year's Eve, the day Carl had to leave for Fort Myers, a day he had not looked forward to, a day filled with regrets. He felt guilty for not spending more time with Tom, Joyce, and Jill—especially, Jill. *At least they gave me the impression they were pleased that I was enjoying myself.—Not being here more than I was, is probably bothering me more than them.—I hope so.*

"Can I help you pack?" Jill asked. "You look as if you're moving in slow motion."

"Thanks, but I'll get it. It's just that I have this feeling if I hurry, the day will go faster."

"Well, let me help you. I'm not anxious for the day to go faster either, but I would like to spend as much of the day in Fort Myers as possible."

"Why?"

"I want to have lunch at the Snack House and…well…you'll see…. Do I look OK? I can't even come close to buttoning my jeans. So I put on this large sweatshirt."

"You look great."

"You won't be embarrassed to be seen with me in public?"

"Not at all. I'll be proud."

As planned, their first stop was the Snack House. The first waiter they saw rushed to greet them. "Hi, Jill. Hi, Carl. Where have you been, Jill?

You don't have to stay away just because Carl joined the Navy." Eventually, all the other waiters joined them at their booth with similar comments. Carl was pleased that he had chosen not to share the Snack House with Sara. His friends, the waiters, would not have been as warm to Jill, and would've shown him little respect.

"I love this place," Jill said. "I'm so glad you introduced me to it." She paused for a moment, "By the way the waiters are acting, you didn't bring 'whoever' here, did you?"

"No. I didn't."

"I hoped you wouldn't…. But, why didn't you?"

He reached for her hand and took it in his. "This is our restaurant."

She held his hand with both of hers, and then, while looking at their hands, she said, "I love you, Carl Sanford."

He was shocked, but when she lifted her eyes to his, he said, "I love you too."

Their eyes didn't move until Jill smiled and asked, "What're you going to have, your usual?"

"Yes. My usual."

He was confused. Was her "I love you" a casual remark, as one family member would say to the other, or did it have more meaning? He wondered if she was just as confused by his reply? The waiter serving their burgers interrupted his thoughts.

While eating, their conversation was directed to how delicious the burgers and fries were, and how long it would be before they returned.

"I have an idea!" Jill said. "Let's come back this evening for dinner."

"Yeah, that's a good idea. What are we going to do between now and then?"

"I need some maternity clothes, and M. Flossie Hill is just down the street. And if they don't have what I want, or something I can afford, there's Sears, J. C. Penney, and Belk Lindsey, all located close together on First Street. If you're embarrassed to go shopping with me, you can drop me off and pick me up later."

"I won't be the least bit embarrassed. But, before we start shopping, let's go drop off my stuff at Ralph's."

Ralph was home with his mother and Frances. Soon after Jill and Carl arrived, the phone rang. Ralph, uncharacteristically, rushed to answer it. "No, he's not here.... I'll be sure to tell him.... That's OK." He glanced at Carl. "Bobby's girlfriend."

By the way Ralph looked and acted, Carl knew it was not Bobby's girlfriend. It was Sara.

"We're going shopping for maternity clothes. Do any of you want to join us?" Jill asked.

Ralph and Frances smiled without answering; they knew she wasn't serious about them going.

"Well," Carl began, "how about joining us for dinner at the Snack House?"

"No thanks. We're going to have dinner here with Mom."

Carl was impressed at how, before buying anything, Jill evaluated the merchandise in all the stores of interest, then returned to make her purchases. She asked his advice on the clothes she tried on; he always gave his honest opinion. It was not his nature to make comments like: "whatever you think," or "if that's what you like," or "if you like it, buy it."

He also admired her excellent, yet conservative, taste. There were a few articles she really wanted, but her funds were limited. He would wait until she was in the dressing room, trying something on, then take the items to the sales lady. She would fold them and put them in the bottom of one of Jill's shopping bags. She always included the receipt so Jill could exchange them.

He even helped pick out baby clothes and toys. Jill's smile and the sparkle in her eyes when she held up a little outfit or a cuddly toy left no doubt that she was looking forward to being a mother.

It was almost dark when they finished shopping, but that didn't keep them from browsing in the many stores on First Street—the same stores Carl and Ralph had explored as children. When they had checked out all the stores of interest, they loaded their many packages in *Blue*. Instead of driving closer to the Snack House, they chose to walk.

Earlier, when they arrived in Fort Myers, and even though Christmas was over and it was New Year's Eve, the town was crowded, and Carl had no choice but to park *Blue* close to the Post Office, which was quite a walk to the Snack House.

"You know," Jill said as she looked up at the massive building, "for a town this size, it sure has a large, beautiful post office."

"I know. To me, it's more than just a building, it's a monument to my grandfather and his perseverance."

"Your father or mother's father?"

"My mother's."

"Why do you think of it as a monument?"

"He dug the basement."

"How'd he do that?"

"With his mule.... Each morning, while working on it, he walked from his home in Tice, a community East of Fort Myers, to the city barn, a distance of about five miles, fed his mule, then rode him here, about three miles. When they arrived, my grandfather hitched a scoop-looking thing to the mule. And all day, with my grandfather holding the handles, the mule would drag the scoop until it filled with dirt, then drag it out for my grandfather to dump. At the end of the day, Granddad would ride the mule back to the barn, feed him, dry him off, and then walk home. This went on for weeks.... Granddad had to be extremely pleased when that job was finished."

"Wow!...That had to be rough. But, I suspect he wasn't as pleased to finish as his mule was."

Carl laughed. "No doubt."

The night was a little chilly, but that didn't seem to bother Jill. She still preferred to walk. They cuddled up close and off they went. *Now, instead of walking the streets of Fort Myers at night with Ralph, it's Jill.*

With Ralph, it was necessary; it was their way to escape the trauma of home. *What a difference!*

"Two times in one day?" the waiter said.

"Yes." Jill answered. "Carl's leaving tomorrow and won't be back for a while. We want our last meal together to be here."

"I'm sorry to hear you're leaving, Carl. But, Jill, that doesn't mean you can't drop in and brighten our establishment."

"Thanks. I'll try."

"What are you going to do with *Blue* while you're away?" the waiter asked.

"Jill will be using her."

"Good," the waiter said. "Then you'll have no excuse for not coming to visit us.... What can I get you guys?"

The waiter took their order, then, as was the custom, rushed to tell the cook before he forgot it. The waiters never wrote anything and never forgot an order.

"I'm going to be using *Blue*?" Jill asked.

"Yes.... While I'm aboard ship, I'll be visualizing you and *Blue* enjoying each other's company, and I'll be comforted by the thought."

"And I'll be thinking of you while driving her." She reached across the table and took his hand in hers. "There's one more place I'd like to go while we're in Fort Myers. I've been looking forward to it ever since I knew I was coming."

"Where?"

"Your special place."

"I've decided it's not my special place any longer."

"Oh, no! Why not?"

"It's 'our' special place."

Her smile expressed her delight, but her eyes became a little watery. "Our special place," she said, her voice a little more than a whisper.

"Are you sure you want to walk out on the dock?" Carl asked when they arrived at the Yacht Basin. "It's pretty cold!"

"I'm sure."

When they reached the end of the dock, they stood side by side with their arms around each other's back, looking out over the river.

"I think the dock is a little too cold to sit on. Don't you?" Carl said.

"Yes, I do."

They were silent for several minutes.

"This is the perfect night," Jill said. "I'll always remember the smell of the river and the sound of its small waves lapping at the pilings and quietly breaking against the shore. And the moon, even though it's only half, look how its yellow reflection goes completely across the river. And I've never seen the sky this clear, or this many stars…. Yes, it's the perfect night…. I meant what I said today at lunch."

"I did too," Carl said without taking his eyes off the river.

"I didn't mean to tell you there. My plan was to tell you here."

As if they had rehearsed the moment, they slowly turned to face each other. She lifted her head, inviting his kiss.

The night was dark, but not so dark that he couldn't see her parted lips move closer to his. He felt and tasted the tears on her trembling lips. It was a kiss filled with emotion, respect, and passion, but mostly, love. Just as he had imagined their first kiss would be.

She pulled away from his lips and pressed her cheek against his chest. "I'm so sorry," she sobbed. "I wish I hadn't married John. I should've listened to you and Tom."

"But, we never said anything negative about John or tried to discourage you from getting married."

"Your eyes did. And I should've paid closer attention to what they were saying."

He ran his fingers up through her short hair and pressed her head close to his chest. "That's all behind us, and there's nothing we can do to change it."

"I know. But I can't believe how dumb I was."

"You weren't dumb, you are honest, and you think everyone else is honest. Your mistake was believing John was being truthful when he wasn't. If he were honest, he would've never gotten such a prize. To win you over, he had to lie and con."

"Looking back, it's hard for me to believe how anxious I was to marry. If I had only waited until one of us was on our own…. It wasn't long after you came to live with us, when I realized I was falling in love, but was afraid to admit my feelings. I was afraid that Tom and Mom would be uncomfortable. They might have even asked you to leave. We talked about it, so I know you felt the same."

"I did. And we should've gone with our feelings."

"That's easy to say now. But I'm not sure Tom and Mom would've agreed."

"They would."

"Why do you think that?"

"Tom told me that he and your mother had always hoped we would fall in love and marry."

They had relaxed their embrace a little while talking, but now her face was pressed even harder against his chest, and she was crying. He wrapped his arms completely around her and pressed his cheek against her hair. He felt as if he could not get close enough.

"I'm so sorry," she sobbed.

"Me, too." The lump in his throat prevented him from saying more.

"What are we going to do?"

"Get married!" he said without the slightest bit of hesitation.

She looked up from his chest. "You're kidding, right?"

"Do I sound like I'm kidding?"

"No, but…"

"You'll be divorced by my next leave. We'll get married then."

She kissed him long and hard. "I love it when you take charge."

"Well?"

"Yes! Yes! Yes! Definitely, yes…. Are you sure?"

"I'm positive."

"So am I." She paused before continuing, "Just that quick, I've gone from the saddest to the happiest moment of my life."

"I feel the same. And it will always be my most memorable…. That was one helluva proposal, wasn't it?"

"It was perfect. Not only was it perfect, I was asked, or," she smiled, "told, in the perfect place…. Our special place."

With their arms around each other, and thinking they could not get close enough, they slowly walked toward town and *Blue*. Neither were in a hurry.

"When is your next leave?" Jill asked.

"I'm not sure. When I return to the *Forrestal*, it'll be leaving for an extended cruise. They tell me it might be a year before it returns."

"Oh, no! I will have delivered by then."

"I know. I wish I could be here for the birth of Tommie, but I can't."

"Tommie," she repeated. "God, I hope it's a girl."

"It will be."

Jill apologized to Ralph and his mother for not being able to stay for the New Year's Eve party they had planned; she would be too late getting home.

Carl leaned in *Blue's* window and kissed her good-bye.

"Happy New Year," they said together.

She waved her cute little wave, and he watched her drive away.

Saying good-bye was not as difficult as they thought it would be. Thinking that getting back to the Navy would make the time go faster, had him anxious to get on with it, and Jill was anxious to get back to Naples and tell her mother and Tom her good news.

"Sara has called at least ten times," Ralph said. "I told her I would have you call as soon as you arrived, but she keeps on calling."

After the first ring she answered.

"Sara?" Carl asked.

"Where have you been? I've been trying to get you since early this afternoon."

"Why? I told you I was spending the rest of my leave with Jill and her family."

"I know. I just want to be with you one more time. Lynette and I are having a New Year's Eve party. Please come over."

"I can't. Ralph is having a party, and I'm invited."

"Can I come to his party, please? I want to be with you."

He realized that giving in to Sara's desires would make him no better than John, and, unlike John, he was not a hypocrite. He was in love, and being honest and true to Jill was the only thing on his mind. He also realized he couldn't let Sara know about his love for Jill and their upcoming marriage. She would tell Lynette, and if Lynette and John got back together she would tell John, then John would have a reason to blame Jill for their marriage failing.

"I'm sorry if I come across as being insensitive, but I'd like to be alone with Ralph and his family."

"I understand. We agreed to go our separate ways and that's what we should do. I guess I was thinking that one more time wouldn't hurt. But, you're right, it wouldn't be right for me to ask you to change your plans or ask to be included. I want you to know that I miss you much more than I thought I would. I also want you to know that I really, really, really enjoyed being with you. I had a great time."

"Meeeee, too."

"Thanks. I needed to know.... Have a happy New Year."

"You, too. And I hope 1958 is good to you."

Ralph had just handed Carl his first glass of eggnog when there was a knock on the door. It was Jill.

"The New Year is only two hours away, and I couldn't bear the thought of not being with you when it arrives."

"I'm glad you came back," Carl said, "but what about your mother and Tom? Aren't they going to worry about you being on the road after midnight?"

"I better call." She looked toward Ralph's mother. "Can I use your phone to make a collect call?"

"Sure," she answered, "but don't make it collect."

"Thanks."

"Wow!" Ralph said to Carl when Jill went to the phone. "That was close."

"Not even a little," Carl replied.

"Uh oh. Do I sense that you and Jill have become more than friends?"

"Yes. We both have known it for a long time, but, out of respect for Tom and her mother, we forced ourselves to restrain from admitting it. Jill was first to reveal how she felt. I followed soon after. It was a wonderful and unforgettable moment. One, I will cherish forever."

"Congratulations. You sure as hell couldn't do better."

"Thanks," Carl said while he and Ralph shook hands. Even though they were alone and on the porch, Carl looked around to be sure no one had seen or heard them. "Please don't tell anyone until her divorce is final."

"Don't worry. I won't."

"Did you tell Ralph we're getting married?" Jill's cheerful voice came from behind them.

Ralph glanced at Carl then opened his arms to Jill. "No, he didn't. But you just did. Congratulations.... Don't worry. I won't complicate your divorce. Your secret is safe with me."

"Thanks.... Mom suggested I spend the night; she doesn't want me driving late at night with all the New Year's celebrations. I asked your mother if she has room. She said she'll make room. Will that be OK with you guys?"

"Sure," Carl said. "I was worried about you driving back tonight."

"Yes," Ralph said. "I agree with your mother. Now you can see us off on the train in the morning."

"That's right!" Jill said while putting her arm around Carl's waist. "I didn't think of that." She paused for a moment, looked up at Carl and said, "I'm so glad I came back."

He kissed her hair. "Me, too."

When Frank Nodine, the radio announcer on WINK, the same announcer Carl and Ralph had grown up listening to, said, "Happy New Year," everyone lifted their glass of eggnog and shouted, "Happy New Year!" After that, Carl and Jill had no idea what the others did; they were too deeply involved with their first kiss of the New Year.

"I have several kinds of pies and ice cream if anyone's interested," Ralph's mother said. Everyone but Carl and Jill took her up on her offer.

"My stomach's not feeling up to par," Carl said. "It's probably nerves. I think a walk in the cool air is what I need."

"I'll join you," Jill said.

The familiar streetlight on the corner of Monroe Street and Victoria Avenue, close to his grandfather's house, was like an old friend. He thought back to the many nights he and his dog, Muggins, had walked away from the light until he could no longer see the sidewalk, then turn and walk back—over and over.

When Carl and Jill walked by his grandfather's house, they looked in; it was dark, which pleased him. He had rather not see someone in it. They continued to the end of the sidewalk, next to the large cypress tree located on the corner of his grandfather's property.

"I can't believe I'm standing with my wife-to-be, under the same tree I climbed as a kid."

Jill leaned against the tree's massive trunk and pulled him close. "Jill Sanford…. I love the way that sounds, and I love you, Carl Sanford."

What started as a gentle kiss, became a kiss filled with love, passion, and desire. It was difficult to suppress their feelings, but standing under a streetlight, for all to see, was not an ideal location. As if they could read the other's mind, they stopped and began walking back to Ralph's.

Carl saw that *Blue* was parked under a tree, in a secluded area. The desire to be with the girl he had loved for years was overwhelming, the same girl who had often shared his bed, but only in his dreams.

The farther they got from the light, the more often they stopped to kiss and caress. Soon they were standing beside *Blue*.

"Will this be safe?" he asked before opening the door.

"Yes. Very safe."

It wasn't long before they were enjoying what each had craved for years. Being aware of Jill's condition, encouraged him to be patient, slow, and easy. Even when Jill began making little sounds of pleasure, he continued to be cautious.

She tightened her arms around his lower waist, so tight he could not move, then lifted her legs even higher and thrust her quivering body against him.

He felt her hands and arms move even lower as she pressed herself against him, forcing him closer. His head felt as if it was about to explode and his ears rang loudly as she squirmed beneath him, but he didn't move.

"Oh…my…God." Her voice was low, so low he could barely make out what she said. "Oh, my…. Oh, my!" she continued.

He couldn't hold back any longer and had no desire to. It was the perfect time.

They held each other for several minutes; neither wanted to move.

"That was a first," she whispered, while kissing his neck.

"The first what? The first time in the back seat of a car?"

"That, too. But, I was referring to my first climax."

He lifted his face above hers. "That was your first?"

"Yes. I came close a few times, but after a while I gave up. John only thought of himself, never me. Sometimes he would finish before he started."

"That had to be bad."

"It was…. But, now that I've experienced how wonderful making love can be, I'm grateful that John never achieved what you did…. God, you're good. I can't wait to do it again…. You ready?"

He laughed. "You know I'm not."

"I was kidding."

"I know. Or, at least I hope you were."

He smiled to himself while putting on his clothes. It pleased him to know that Jill had experienced her first with him, not John.

Both of Jill's arms were in her sweater and she was about to pull it over her head when she noticed that Carl had moved closer. She stopped when his lips touched hers, and even though their kiss had intensified, she managed to remove one arm from her sweater, which exposed her breast. As he positioned the nipple of her breast in the palm of his hand, a tingling sensation radiated through her whole body, especially, when he removed his lips from hers and slowly kissed his way to her chest.

A surge of pleasure rushed through her as his hand tightened around her breast, and the quivering in her lower belly increased when he slowly placed his mouth over her hard, excited nipple. She closed her eyes and visualized it being sucked deep into his mouth.

While slowly moving his lips to her other breast, he paused and lifted his head. Jill opened her eyes; she had not heard anything, but sensed he had.

"What was that?" she asked.

"I don't know." He looked in the direction he heard the sound. "It was a couple talking as they walked by. But we better go in before someone comes looking for us."

She agreed.

"Feel better?" Ralph's mother asked.

"Much better," Carl answered. "I just needed a walk in the fresh air."

"You can sleep in Bobby's old room," Ralph's mother said to Jill. "Carl usually sleeps there, but I fixed the couch for him."

"Thanks. I hope my staying here hasn't caused you any extra work."

"Heaven's no. I feel much more comfortable knowing you're here rather than being on the road with all those drunks. I figured you didn't have anything to sleep in, so I got you one of my granny gowns. It's not too stylish, but it's warm."

"This will be great. Thanks."

Not long after Bobby and his girlfriend left and Ralph took Frances home, Ralph's mother, Jill, and Carl called it a night.

Carl couldn't sleep. His thoughts were keeping him awake. He thought about Jill in the next room and wondered if she was also having trouble sleeping. He thought about his commitment to the Navy and how much he didn't want to return. It bothered him to know he would not be home when Jill had her baby.

He was thinking about his and Jill's love and how foolish they had been for concealing it when he felt her easing under his covers. They kissed, and without saying a word, she turned her back to him; he put his arm over her and they snuggled close. It didn't take but a few minutes before both were sleeping.

Chapter 13

▼

Surprisingly, traffic was light for the first day of a new year, which allowed Jill to think about her and Carl's last days together. Her most dominating thought was Carl's sad look as he waved from the window of the train when it began to move. With her eyes fixed on his and with one hand covering her mouth and waving with the other, she had walked beside his moving window to the end of the station. The last she saw of him was his hand pressed against his window. She waved until she could no longer make out which window was his. It was a sad memory. One she knew would last forever.

The only sound was the steady purr of *Blue's* smooth-running engine, which Jill concentrated on to take her mind off how much she already missed her future husband. She felt even closer when she thought how he trusted her to use and care for his pride and joy. She had always admired the way Carl talked to his car as if it were a person, the most important person in his life.

"Don't worry, *Blue*. I'm not going to come between you and Carl. I only want to be a part of your lives." She smiled when she realized that, for the first time, she had spoken to *Blue*. It was a bonding experience.

What a wonderful start to a new year. Last night, soon after twelve, I had sex, wonderful sex I might add, with the man I plan to be with for the rest of my life, then slept with him, and now I'm driving his car home to tell Mom and Tom of our plans to marry. They'll be so pleased.

A quick glance to the back seat brought back the memory of the night before. *I know I'm not the first to enjoy that seat—there have been several others. I regret its reputation, but I'm pleased to know that I'm the last. If Carl and I had dated, the seat would not have the reputation it has, Carl and I would've married, and the baby I'm carrying would be his.—It's my own fault.—I was the one who suggested to Carl that we control our desire to be more than friends. That was a mistake. Another mistake was concealing my feelings from Mom.—From what Carl said, I feel certain that both Mom and Tom would not have discouraged us from dating.—I should've talked with her.*

Yes, I've made some mistakes, but my worst was marrying John. I can't believe I didn't see how deceitful he was. Everyone else did.—Carl tried to warn me.—I wish I had given more thought to what he said the day before he left for the Navy. Seeing the tears in his eyes when I left him standing in front of Ralph's house should've inspired me to drive back and have an honest talk about our feelings. I remember, while driving back to Naples, my thoughts were about Carl, not John, and I came close to turning around. "God! I wish I had."

As expected, Jill's mother and Tom were extremely pleased to hear that she and Carl had finally admitted to the love they had suppressed. They were even more pleased and excited when she told them that she and Carl planned to marry. The phone interrupted their rejoicing. Jill answered it.

A chill ran through her when she heard: "This is John's father." She wondered what he was going to accuse her of now. She didn't have long to wait.

There was always a sarcastic tone to his voice when he spoke to her, but this time was even more. "You will no longer have to concern yourself with a divorce." Without giving Jill an opportunity to comment, he continued, "I've just been informed by the Fort Myers police department of John's death."

"Oh my God!" she screamed. "What happened?"

"All I know is he had been drinking, which he would've never started if it wasn't for you. He probably thought alcohol would help him get over how unfaithful you were."

"How can you say that?" she cried.

"Because it's true. We were a close family, with a loving, caring son until you came into our lives. I blame you for his death. And, my wife and I had rather not see you at his funeral. So, try to be a little considerate and not attend."

"But..."

Tom and her mother moved close, one on either side. She slowly hung up the phone, then reached for her mother.

"What was that all about?" Tom asked.

"That was John's father," she sobbed. "John died last night, and he blames me for his death."

"How can he think you had anything to do with John's death?" Joyce asked.

"He said John was drinking, which, according to him, John would never do if he hadn't met me."

"Did he have an accident while driving?" Tom asked.

"I don't know. He hung up before I could ask. But he did say he was informed by the Fort Myers Police Department. So I guess whatever happened to him happened in Fort Myers."

"The police chief and I are good friends," Tom said. "I'll give him a call." He used the phone in the kitchen, where the phone book was.

Grief was Jill's first emotion, but her sorrow soon changed to anger when she thought about what John's father had said.

"John's father doesn't want me to attend John's funeral."

Joyce looked at her as if she had misunderstood. "He doesn't want you to be at John's funeral!"

"He asked me to be considerate and not attend."

"Be considerate!..."

"Did I hear you right?" Tom interrupted. He had finished his call. "That asshole asked you to not attend John's funeral?"

"That's what he said."

"If you want to go, we'll go. And I don't give a damn what that idiot says."

"Right now, I don't know what I want."

"Well, before you make a decision, let me tell you what the chief said: John was at a New Year's Eve party, drinking and showing-off. The people at the party said he downed a whole fifth of vodka, then went outside. They thought he was going out to throw up, but he didn't return. The chief said no one seemed concerned. They were just pleased he left.

"It was almost daylight before someone found him passed out in the back seat of his car. They rushed him to the hospital, but he died soon after. The doctor said it was alcohol poisoning."

"How can John's father blame me for that?"

"He has to blame someone," Tom answered. "He's certainly not going to admit that his son was anything but perfect."

"I think I'd rather not go to his funeral," Jill said. "If I go, his father will only humiliate me, and I don't need to deal with any more of his sarcastic remarks. I just want to get on with my life and forget John, and his father. This is the first time since soon after I married John that I've been truly happy, and I don't want anything or anyone to distract me from enjoying being pregnant and loving Carl.

"My friends will wonder why I didn't go. Those that are close will ask, and I'll tell them. The others, I don't care what they think."

"You won't have to tell but one," Joyce said. "In this small town, news travels fast."

"Are you sure?" Tom asked. "Out of respect for your baby's father, don't you think you should be there?"

She thought about what Tom said before answering, "You're right. I should be there." She looked at her mother then Tom. "Will you go with me?"

"Yes," they answered, and at the same time. "We'll be with you."

Jill dealt with John's death surprisingly well. His infidelity and lies had destroyed the love she once had for him. Now she had to deal with his arrogant father.

While eulogizing his son, John's father portrayed him as the perfect child, an athletic teenager, and an ambitious adult. Jill, Tom, and her mother were sitting in the front pew, not with the family, but close. As

John's father continued reading from his prepared eulogy, Jill saw that Tom was becoming extremely irritated. She hoped he could control his temper.

Tom was silent until "The Preacher," as Tom called him, looked toward Jill and said: "The only mistake John made, was marrying outside the church." Tom was still in control until he added, "John tried to be a good husband, but found it difficult to please."

When Tom stood, Jill knew he had lost control. "What the hell do you think you're doing!" Tom shouted. "Do you think I'm going to sit here and listen to you humiliate my daughter?...I know now why you didn't want her to attend her husband's funeral!" Tom was shaking with anger. "Your son was not the man you have described, and I'm not going to let you sacrifice my daughter just to make him look like the perfect husband!" His anger continued to build. "I realize this is not the place for me to express how I feel about your son, but I also realize it's not the place, or the time, for you to accuse my daughter of being a difficult wife!" He was silent for a moment, then looked down at his wife and Jill. "Let's get out of here." He offered his hand to Jill, and then his wife.

With Jill on one side of Tom and her mother on the other, they walked arm in arm toward the door. Jill tried to keep from looking at the people who attended the service, but couldn't help but notice that some were beginning to stand as she and her family walked out. Once outside and walking toward their car, Jill looked back. She was surprised, but pleased to see that most of the people were leaving.

A few months later, Jill's ex father-in-law was replaced with a new minister.

* * * *

It was the first week of July when the *Forrestal* docked at Mayport Florida for some unscheduled maintenance. It would be in port for two weeks. Carl and Ralph asked for a two-week leave, but were allowed only one. Not long after the *Forrestal* was secured, they left for the train station in

Jacksonville. Without informing anyone of their arrival, they boarded the night train to Fort Myers. They slept most of the way.

The train arrived early the next morning, and since their luggage was light, they walked to Ralph's house. They were going to be home less than a week, so they had packed only a few things.

It took a moment for Ralph's mother to regain her composure after awakening to find her son, dressed in his uniform, standing beside her bed. After Ralph and his mother embraced, she put on her robe and went into the living room and hugged Carl.

"Can I fix you boys some breakfast?"

"No thanks, Mom. Carl is anxious to see Jill. He says she's having some problems with her pregnancy."

While Ralph called Frances, to let her know he was in town and ask if she would like to ride to Naples, his mother asked Carl if Jill's condition was serious.

"I'm not sure. In her last letter she said her doctor ordered her to stay in bed for the remainder of her pregnancy."

"When is she due?"

"The last of July."

"Well," Ralph said when he entered the room. "Frances has to work. So I won't see her until later today…. You ready?" he asked Carl.

"Don't you want to change clothes?" Carl asked.

"Not really. I'll change when I get back."

Carl figured that Ralph was concerned about getting him to Jill as soon as possible.

Jill was just as shocked to see Carl walking into her bedroom, as Ralph's mother was to see Ralph. "Carl!" she screamed.

He rushed to take her in his arms. They embraced and kissed without talking.

"How are you feeling?" he asked.

"I feel fine as long as I stay in bed." She wiped the tears from her eyes and face, then pressed her lips to his. "I miss you."

"No more than I miss you."

"How did you get a leave? I didn't expect to see you until after…"

"Let me say it for you." He raised his head a little and looked her in the eyes. "Until after the birth of 'our' baby."

"I'm so happy," she sobbed, then pulled him back against her chest.

Without moving, he asked, "Can you get out of bed at all, or are you confined to it?"

"I'm allowed to get out for a little while each day."

"Long enough to apply for a marriage license and get a blood test?"

"You betcha!"

"Today?"

"The sooner the better."

"Are you sure you don't want to wait and have a large, more official wedding?"

"I had one of those. All I want is you. And I don't care if you have to roll me into the courthouse in a wheelbarrow to get our license…. How long is your leave?"

"One week."

"We better hurry."

"Are you sure?"

"I'm positive!"

"I'll go tell your mother and Ralph."

"Joyce, Ralph…. Jill and I have some news we want to share," Carl said when he entered the living room. "Even though I'm going to be here for only a week, and Jill is limited to the amount of time she can be out of bed, we plan to get married before I return."

"Oh, Carl," Joyce said. "That's the best news I've heard in months. I'm so happy I could kiss you…. I think I will." She stood, and while they embraced, she kissed him on the cheek. "I can just imagine how excited and thrilled Jill is. I better go calm her down."

"Congratulations," Ralph said while offering his hand. They shook with their right and embraced with their left. "Have you picked a day?"

"Let's see…. Today is Monday. I don't know if she'll feel like doing much today?"

"Yes, I do!" Jill yelled from her bedroom.

And then Joyce yelled, "You guys come in here and let's figure out a day."

"Hi, Jill," Ralph said as he leaned down to hug her.

"You're looking good," Jill said. "Why are you and Carl dressed in your uniforms?"

"We were kinda in a hurry."

"Thanks, Ralph. You're a good friend. I wish I had grown up with a friend like you.... OK, let's plan a day. First, we need to apply for a marriage license and get a blood test; it'll take three days before we can pick up the license. This is Monday," then lowering her voice, "Tuesday, Wednesday, Thursday.... Let's say Friday, just to be sure." She looked up at Ralph, "Is Friday good for you and Frances?"

"If it's in the evening. Frances has to work during the day."

"We'll have it in the evening. And guess what?"

"I give up," Ralph answered.

"Friday is Carl's nineteenth birthday."

"Well, how 'bout that."

"So," Joyce began, "the wedding will be here, on Friday, say about eight o'clock. I'm sure Tom can get his friend, Judge Stanley, to perform the ceremony.... Do we have a plan?"

"Sounds like a plan to me," Carl said.

Everyone agreed.

Carl and Joyce were careful not to let Jill overexert herself when they went for the marriage license and blood test. Everything went well, but as soon as they returned home, Joyce insisted that Jill return to bed. Joyce fixed them a sandwich and served it to them in Jill's room. After eating, and returning their plates to the kitchen, Carl lay beside her. It wasn't long before both were asleep.

Joyce met Tom at the door with her finger across her lips. "Be real quiet," she whispered, then took his hand and led him to the door of Jill's room. Jill was sleeping on her back and Carl was on his side with his arm across her.

"When did Carl come home?" he whispered.

Still holding his hand, she eased him away from the door. "He arrived early this morning. He'll be here for a week. And guess what?"

"What?"

"Carl, Jill, and I drove to town today." She watched his curiosity build. "They applied for a marriage license and got a blood test." She placed her hand over his mouth before telling him the rest. "And, Friday, we're going to have a wedding." She removed her hand, revealing a large smile. Instead of shouting, like she thought he would, he opened his arms, wrapped them around her waist, and picked her up. With her head above his and her arms around his neck, they kissed.

They continued to kiss as he relaxed his arms, allowing her to slowly slide down his chest until her feet touched the floor.

"That's the best news I've heard in weeks," Tom said.

"That's what I said. Only I said, months."

"Mom!" Jill called from her room. "Is that Tom I hear?"

Joyce didn't answer; Tom was already rushing to her. "Hi, Baby."

"Did Mom tell you?"

"Yes, she did," he kissed her on the cheek, "and I couldn't be happier. What a surprise."

"It was Carl's idea."

"Well, it was a good one."

Tom looked over at Carl—he was waking. He rushed to the other side of the bed, and before Carl was completely awake, he was shaking his hand. He pulled him to a sitting position and put his large arms around him. "Congratulations."

Tom was eager to bring Carl up to date on all the things that had happened. So, while Joyce helped Jill to the bathroom, they went into the living room. Most everything Tom mentioned, Jill had told him in her letters, but he enjoyed hearing it again.

Jill had dinner with them, but soon after, returned to her bed. Carl helped clean off the table before joining Jill in her bedroom—Joyce and Tom had refused his offer to help wash the dishes. When Tom and Joyce finished in the kitchen, they joined Carl and Jill. Joyce sat on the bed beside Jill, and Tom sat next to Carl. They talked until Tom stood and said it was time for him to hit the sack.

Carl swung his legs off the bed. "I guess it's time for me to check out my bed."

"Oh, no you're not!" Jill said. "You're sleeping with me! There's no way I can sleep knowing you're sleeping in the next room."

"But, I'm afraid I might roll over and hurt you. And…and…" He looked to Joyce and Tom for a sign.

"I think you should sleep in here," Joyce said, "otherwise, she'll be sleeping with you in your bed, and it's too small."

Tom agreed.

Carl prepared for bed then eased under the covers. They kissed and caressed for a while, then she encouraged him to lie on his side with his back to her. He fell asleep with their baby kicking his back.

Sometime during the night, she rolled onto her other side; he turned with her, and for the rest of the night, if one turned, the other turned. That night a pattern was established. One that would last throughout their lives.

Chapter 14

▼

Not far from the Mediterranean, Carl received a message: MOM AND TOMMIE ARE DOING GREAT—WE MISS YOU—JOYCE. It was dated July 25, 1958. He rushed to find Ralph.

"I'm a father!"

"How's Jill?" Ralph asked.

"Joyce said she's doing great."

"Well, congratulations." They shook hands and hugged.

In the letter he received a few weeks later, Jill described, in detail, every phase of Tommie's birth: how cute she was, how much she weighed, and the problems with her delivery. "I controlled my emotions," she wrote, "until I read Tommie's birth certificate: Father: Carl Henry Sanford. I cried and so did Mom." His eyes filled with tears.

Carl's letters to his mother kept her informed of his and Jill's lives. She knew of Jill's marriage to John and her plans to divorce him even though she was pregnant. He wrote her when John passed away, again when he and Jill married, and had informed her of Tommie's birth.

On his next leave, six months after Tommie's birth, he and Jill drove to Fort Myers to visit her. He was surprised at how little affection she showed Tommie and Jill. They decided the reason for her behavior was because Jill had married someone before Carl, and Tommie was not his biological daughter.

Their visit with his mother didn't go well, but the rest of his three-week leave was wonderful. He spent every minute he could with Tommie. If she was awake, he was doing something with her; when she slept, and Joyce and Tom were not around, he and Jill made love.

Carl had missed his daughter's first Christmas, but was certain he would be home for his and Jill's anniversary and Tommie's first birthday.

*   *   *   *

As planned, Carl arrived a day before his birthday and anniversary. For an anniversary present, Tom had not chartered his boat and it was fueled up and ready to go; he and Joyce would keep Tommie. It was Jill's first time away from her daughter.

Carl and Jill left about midmorning; they planned to return the following morning. With both sitting behind the helm, in the captain's seat, they motored to Little Marco Island. It was the middle of the week; the island was deserted, with no other boat in sight. After making sure the anchor was set, they made love. When they woke, they had a light snack. Joyce had prepared a basket of wonderful food.

They inflated the raft, loaded it with the basket of food, drinks, and a blanket, then paddled ashore. It was a short walk across the island to the Gulf, and when they arrived, there was no one on the beach for as far as they could see in either direction.

A light breeze was blowing off the Gulf, just enough to cool the warm day and make spreading the blanket easy. To keep the blanket from blowing away, they placed the basket and drinks on it. Then, without either suggesting it, they took off their swimsuits and ran for the water.

When they tired of swimming and playing they returned to the blanket. Still nude, they began to pet, and it wasn't long before they were making love.

Surprisingly, for July, the weather was comfortable, and as the sun began to set, it even became a little cool. They put on their swimsuits and had something to eat and drink, then held each other and watched the most beautiful sunset they had ever seen—certainly the most memorable.

By the time they returned to the boat, it was getting dark. Soon after deflating the raft and stowing it, they went below and showered, chose a berth, kissed, and cuddled in their favorite sleeping position—him snuggled up close behind her with his chest tight against her back and his hand comfortably caressing her breast. He tightened his hand and said, "Good night, Hon.... I love you."

She placed her hand on his and said, "I love you too.... Good night." That was another custom performed the rest of their lives.

At the same time Carl opened his eyes, he felt Jill move. "What was that?" she asked.

"Thunder."

He tightened his arm around her and waited for the next clap of thunder; he wanted to get an idea of how close the squall line was. He didn't have to wait long.

She was rubbing the back of his hand, the one holding her breast, when the cabin ignited with the illuminance of what seemed like a hundred flash bulbs. There was not even a second between the flash of light and the thunder. Neither flinched; they were accustomed to lightning and the thunder that followed.

"Wow!" Jill said. "That was close."

"Yes it was. We better go out and check the weather."

The wind began to howl, and about the time Carl got his pants on and Jill one of his long shirts, the boat rocked from a violent gust of wind.

Carl opened the companionway door and they stepped out into the cockpit. "I'm afraid it's going to be a bad one," he said.

"Do you think the anchor will hold?"

"Depends on how strong the wind gets. If the wind picks up, the anchor won't hold. The bottom is too hard to hold the type anchor we have out."

Since the boat was on the lee side of the island, the waves would not be a problem, but the wind would. Their worst fear was running aground. The distance between the island and mainland was quite narrow.

The wind intensified, and without saying a word, Jill started the engines while Carl went below to get the hand-held searchlight. Even before he returned, the wind struck with a raging force, and the rain fell as if the sky had burst.

"I'm going to stand on the bow pulpit!" he shouted above the screaming wind. "I'll shine the light in the direction of the anchor. Hopefully, you'll be able to see the beam of light through the rain." He knew there was no need to explain to her that she was to keep the boat pointed toward the anchor and with just enough speed to take some of the tension off the anchor line.

"If I shine the light straight up, that means you're going too fast and we definitely don't want the line in the propellers."

"I understand…. Aren't you going to put on some foul-weather gear?"

"There's no time."

As Carl made his way forward, Jill struggled to open the windshield. With rain that hard, she knew the windshield wipers would be of little use. Even though the boat wasn't headed directly into the wind, the windshield was still difficult to open. When she managed to overpower the wind, she pushed the windshield open enough to see under the bottom edge, then locked the lifter and began concentrating on where Carl was shining the light. He was shining it to his left.

She turned the wheel hard to port, but the bow didn't move; the wind was too strong and the anchor was dragging. When she noticed the boat was not responding, she put the port engine in reverse and left the starboard engine in forward, then increased the speed of both. She watched the beam of light slowly move to forward as the boat began to face the wind.

Once the light was pointed dead ahead, she put both engines in forward and adjusted the speed to match the wind. Now, with the boat headed into the wind, the force of the freezing rain was blowing in the open windshield, which caused her to struggle to keep her eyes open, but that was still better than trying to see through a blurry windshield. She wondered how Carl, dressed only in a pair of trousers, was enduring the cold. She was trembling so much she could hardly stand.

The squall lasted about fifteen minutes—a long fifteen minutes. When the wind died enough for the anchor to hold, Carl left the pulpit. Jill shut down the engines and closed the windshield.

To keep from getting the inside of the cabin wet, they took their clothes off in the cockpit.

"There's nothing like getting out of a warm bed to go stand in the freezing rain of a summer squall," Carl said.

"Just another cherished memory," Jill said while removing her shirt.

They were completely naked when Jill turned the cabin light on. "Oh, Hon!" she said. "Your lips are blue."

"So are yours."

She added a blanket to their berth, pulled it back and got in. He turned the light off and joined her.

"My God you're freezing!" she said when she felt his cold body against hers. She was on her back. He was on his side with a leg and arm across her. "How are we ever going to get warm?"

"I don't know?" he said. He positioned his face above hers then kissed her cold lips.

"From the movement I feel against my leg, I think you do."

It wasn't long before being cold was far removed from their thoughts.

Chapter 15

"It's for you," Joyce said as she called Carl to the phone.

He and Jill were on the living room floor playing with Tommie. They had not been home long from their cruise to Little Marco.

"Carl, this is Snag Thompson."

"Hi, Snag. How are you?" He tried to act nonchalant, but he knew when the Lee County Sheriff calls, there's a problem. The sheriff's first name was Flanders, but he preferred to be called "Snag."

"I'm doing fine. But I'm afraid your mother is in a little trouble."

"What kind of trouble?"

"She's written a bad check."

"Oh my God!...How can that be?"

"I don't know. She even wrote it to the same man she wrote the last one to. I guess he figured there was no way she would do it twice."

"But, Snag!...You can't believe how much money she's gone through. If that's what's happened."

"I've known your mother a long time, and nothing she does surprises me."

"How much did she write it for this time?"

"The same as the last: one hundred."

"Is the fine still fifty?"

"I'm sorry, but yes.... When the jailer asked her who she wanted to call, she gave him your number. And since you live in Naples, and it's a long distance call, he couldn't call. That's why I'm calling."

"Have you talked with her?" Carl asked.

"No, not yet. I don't think I want to."

"I understand.... It's still early. I'll be there within the hour."

"There's no need to hurry.... Is Tom around?"

"He just left for his boat to put some supplies on board. He has a charter early tomorrow morning."

"Tell him I said 'hello.' And good luck with your mother. I wish there was something I could do."

"I'll tell Tom you called. And thanks for your concern. I want you to know that I appreciate all you've done for me. I'm not sure what would've happened to me after Dad's death if it wasn't for your help and guidance."

"As you know, your dad, Tom, and I grew up together, went to the same schools, and dated some of the same girls. They even campaigned for me during my first election. Your dad was one of the finest men I've ever known. I'm sure you understand when I say your mother didn't deserve him. I also want to say that I think you've done an excellent job of dealing with the hand you were dealt. Your mother sure as hell didn't make it easy for you. I only found out today that you're living with Tom, and I couldn't be more pleased."

"I couldn't be happier, and thanks for calling, Snag." Carl had no idea why the sheriff was called "Snag," but everyone did, and he had never heard him called by any other name—not even during his elections.

There had to be a reason, he thought, for her to write a check without sufficient funds. It was difficult for him to believe that she had spent, or wasted, the money she received from Don's estate—especially, while renting the two apartments in his grandfather's house and the efficiency apartment behind Don's house.

By the sound of Carl's conversation, Jill knew his mother was in trouble. "What's she done now?"

"She wrote another worthless check."

"Oh, my God! I can't..." She stopped so Carl wouldn't know how upset she was.

"Do you feel up to taking a ride to Fort Myers?" he asked.

"Yes. I think I should. You might be late, and you'll need someone to keep you awake.... I'll get Tommie ready."

When they arrived at the Lee County Jail, Jill chose to wait in *Blue* while Carl went in.

"Do you have the money to bail her out?" the jailer asked when Carl asked to see his mother.

"Yes, I have the money." He sort of misled the jailer; he had the money, but he wasn't planning to use it.

The jailer pointed to one of the chairs at a table and motioned for Carl to have a seat. "I'll get her."

"Get me out of here, NOW!" she shouted when she entered the room.

Carl knew the image of the anger her eyes reflected, the rage in her voice, and the hurt he felt would take a long time to get over, if ever.

The jailer motioned for her to sit in the chair opposite Carl.

"Can you believe that man had me arrested and put in here?" she shouted.

"You put yourself in here!" the jailer said.

Instantly, Carl formed an opinion of the jailer—he didn't like him.

"Just give him the money," his mother shouted, "and get me out of here!"

"I can't afford to lose $150.00 dollars. You never paid me back from the last time I bailed you out."

"What are you talking about? Frank took care of that problem."

"Frank took the credit, but I'm the one, thanks to Ralph and Bobby, who came up with the money."

"Whatever!...That was then, this is now. So pay the man, and I'll pay you when we get home."

"If you have money, why did you write a bad check?"

"Wait just a damn minute!" the jailer shouted. "I didn't bring her out here so the two of you can carry on a conversation! Either you show me $150.00 or I'm locking her up."

Tears formed in his mother's eyes, and her chin began to tremble. "Please, Carl," she sobbed. "Please don't let him take me back to that cell with those crazy women."

Carl was reaching for his wallet when the sheriff walked in. He glanced at Carl, then glared at the jailer. "I've heard about all I need to hear of your smart mouth," he said to the jailer. His eyes were dancing with anger. "Do you have her in the cell with the drunks and whores?"

"Well, yes."

"I can't believe you did that." He shook his head in disbelief. "I know this young man and, under the circumstances, he's doing the best he can, and I expect they need some privacy while they figure this out. And they sure as hell aren't a threat to the security of this jail. So wait in the next room. They'll let you know what they decide.

"And if he has to leave to get the money, don't give him a hard time when he returns. And, you damn sure better not put her back in that same cell."

After giving Carl a sympathetic look, and without as much as a glance toward his mother, the sheriff left the room.

The jailer was not even out of the room before his mother began disciplining him. "You have your nerve. Building me up to think you came here to get me out; now you're accusing me of not having any money. I have money and plenty of it. It's invested and I can't get it for a while."

"What's it invested in?"

"That's none of your business!"

"I don't believe you. I think you've gone through all Don's money, and now you think you can demand me to part with some of mine. You didn't appreciate Don and you've never appreciated me, so if you can't think of someone or some place I can get the money, you can stay here. I hate to say that, but after the way you treated Don, and then his son, I lost what little respect I had for you. And, I'm not going to let you screw up my life any more than you have."

"After all I've done for you, and this is the thanks I get!" She paused for a moment, letting what Carl said sink in. "Eddie will help me. Go get the money from him."

"Why didn't you ask the jailer to call him instead of me?"

"Because he got married a few months ago."

"Married! I thought you and he had something going and were going to be partners."

"We're still partners. He just doesn't want his new wife to know."

"Why's that?"

"He says she's real jealous. But, as long as he pays me what he owes me, it doesn't matter."

"Did you pay for that new truck I saw?"

"Yes, and a lot more."

"Has he paid you for the truck or anything else you bought him?"

"Not yet. But he will as soon as his company starts making money."

"I'll bet…. Where does he live?"

"Edison Park."

"Nice area."

"That's where his wife lived when they married."

He got the directions and left.

On the way to Eddie's, Carl and Jill discussed his experience with his mother. He mentioned how angry he got, yet how sorry he felt for her.

"She is a very sick woman," Jill said.

"You're right. For a person to be as inconsiderate as my mother, they'd have to be sick. If only there was something I could do to help."

"You've done all you can, a lot more than most. Now, you have to think about your own life. If you continue to come to her aid, she'll use and abuse you; just like she did your father, Don, and Donnie." She smiled as she turned her head toward him. "I know you didn't ask for my advice, but you got it."

"I value your advice, and don't ever be afraid to give it…. And, you're right, but it's awfully difficult to put her out of my mind. It's as if I'm abandoning her."

"It's hard to imagine how much you've suffered, yet you still have compassion for her…. I'm so glad you're not like her."

Carl pulled *Blue* close to the curb in front of Eddie's elegant house. "Would you like to come in?"

"No thanks. I'll wait for you."

Carl realized that controlling his temper while talking with Eddie would be difficult, but he had to try.

Eddie recognized Carl, but didn't speak; he just held the door open and stared.

"I hate to drop by without calling first, but Mom's in trouble and needs a little help."

Eddie was in a predicament, and Carl enjoyed seeing him squirm.

"What kind of trouble?"

"She wrote a check without sufficient funds, and the man she wrote it to had her arrested."

"So…. What do you want me to do about it?"

"You told me, when I saw you at Don's, that you and Mom were starting a business and she bought the new truck I saw. Besides the truck, she said she invested a lot more money in your company."

"I guess you believe her and think I should bail her out?"

"In this case, yes, I believe her, and I think the least you can do is get her out."

"Look. Your mother bought me the truck as a gift. You know what I mean?"

"I know you conned her by telling her she was a partner. You even told me she was your partner."

"I'll show you."

Carl followed him, even though he was not invited.

Eddie pulled out a desk drawer, removed an envelope, and handed it to Carl. "This is the title, and it's in my name and my name only."

Carl looked at it. Eddie was right.

"And as far as me owing her additional money, there's not a piece of paper with my name on it stating that I owe her a dime." He took the title from Carl. "Now, get out of my house before my wife gets home. She doesn't know I dated your mother, and I don't want her to find out."

Eddie opened the door, but Carl didn't move.

"I said, get out!" he shouted.

"I don't think so," Carl calmly said. "I'll go when your wife arrives."

"You better leave now, or…"

"Or what? It sounds to me like you were about to threaten to throw me out. Believe me, there's nothing more I'd like than for you to try. So, I think the wise thing for you to do, if you don't have cash, is get your checkbook."

Eddie went back to his desk and took out his checkbook. "How much will it take to get her out?"

"It'll take $150.00, but since this is the last money Mom can expect to get, make the check out for $500.00."

"What! That's blackmail!"

"I don't care what you call it, just write the damn check!"

"I'm not about to!"

"Fine. When your wife and I finish with you, you'll wish you'd written it for $5,000.00."

Eddie began to write. "I'm going to make it out to you, that way my wife will think it's a loan."

Carl didn't answer.

Lights flashed across the living room windows.

"That's my wife," Eddie said. "Here, take this and put it in your pocket or some place."

Carl looked at the check, then folded it and put it in his shirt pocket.

"Ed!" his wife shouted. "Do you know there's an old car with a young lady and baby parked out front?" When she moved from the foyer to the living room, she spotted Carl. "Oh, I'm sorry. I didn't know you had company."

Carl and Eddie's wife waited to be introduced, but Eddie didn't take his eyes off the floor.

"This fellow stopped by looking for work." Eddie rushed to open the door. "He was just leaving."

"I have a job," Carl said to Eddie's wife. "I'm in the Navy. And I'm damn sure not here looking for work. Especially, not with this lying gigolo." While passing Eddie in the doorway, he paused long enough to say, "Now, you son of a bitch, how are you going to explain that?"

On the way back to the jail, Carl explained how he had encouraged Eddie to write a check for $500.00 instead of $150.00. He was silent for a few moments. "I have a problem."

"I know," Jill said.

"You do?"

"Yes.... You're worried that if you give her the extra money, she'll blow it. And if you keep it, you'll feel guilty. Right?"

"Right.... What should I do?"

She thought for a moment. "I suggest, after you bail her out, you keep the $150.00 you told me she owes you from the last time you bailed her out, and give her the rest. We both know she'll waste it, but it's hers to waste."

"Have I told you today that I love you?"

"A few times, but tell me again."

Carl's mother was at the table waiting for him. The jailer had seen him drive up.

"Do you have the money?" the jailer asked.

"Yes."

He handed the jailer $150.00 and the jailer gave his mother her purse.

"I'll wait for you outside," his mother said. "I need a cigarette."

When the jailer finished writing the receipt, Carl joined his mother outside.

"I talked Eddie into writing a check for $500.00," he said. "As soon as I cash it, I'll keep the one-fifty you owe me from before, the one-fifty for this time, and give you the balance."

"I can't believe that you let me stay in that God-awful place when all the time you had the money in your pocket!" She slapped her cigarette to her lips, then blew the smoke out of the corner of her mouth. "Is the check made out to me?"

"No. It's made out to me."

"Well, sign it and I'll send you your precious money."

"Not a chance."

"After all I've done for you, this is the respect I get."

"I'm getting damn tired of hearing 'after all I've done for you.' All you've done for me is make my life a living hell."

"If that's the way you feel, just keep the money!...Take me home!"

Jill and Tommie had moved to the back.

"Hi, Lois."

She didn't answer.

Chapter 16

▼

While returning to Naples, Jill asked, "If your mother has spent all the money Don left her, do you think she's behind on the house payment?"

"Probably. I better call Marcie and find out."

"Marcie? Who's Marcie?"

"She's the president of the bank. She and my father's family were close. Tom and I still are. Not only do we call her by her first name, so does everyone who is a customer at her bank. She insists they do."

When Carl called Marcie, he was shocked to find that his mother was ten months behind on her payments. Four hundred dollars.

"I'm glad you called," Marcie said. "I was just getting ready to call Tom to see if he knew how I could get in touch with you. I've been patient with your mother for as long as I can, much longer than I should. But I know your Dad wouldn't want you to lose your grandfather's house."

"Thanks. I really appreciate that."

"If you can make the payments, I suggest you convince your mother to put the house in your name. If you don't, she'll sell it to keep it from going into foreclosure, and by the way she's letting it depreciate, she won't get much more than the mortgage and back payments. I hate to say it, but if something isn't done soon I'll have no choice but to foreclose. And once I turn it over to the attorneys, the house won't be worth the attorney fees, the court cost, and the payments she's behind on. You'll be left with nothing."

"How should I go about getting her to agree to signing the house over to me?"

"Tell her you talked with me and I'm going to foreclose, which is true. Then tell her if I do foreclose, neither of you will have anything, which is also true. Do you have four hundred?"

"Yes, but that's about all."

"Offer her the four hundred and tell her you'll also pay the four hundred she owes, but she'll have to put the house in your name. I'll add the four hundred in back payments to the mortgage. I'll also have the bank's attorneys take care of the paperwork. Since you are a minor, do you think you can get Tom to cosign?"

"I'm sure he would. He's not too pleased with knowing Mom could lose his father's house.... Did you know that his stepdaughter and I are married?"

"Well, congratulations. No, I didn't know. It seems like yesterday when your dad brought you in to open a savings account. Do you still have the account?"

"Yes, I do."

"Good luck with your mother, and let me know something as soon as you can."

"I will, and thanks for everything."

He and Jill left for Fort Myers that afternoon.

"What do you mean, you want me to give you my house!" his mother shouted.

"I didn't say that. And besides, it's as much my house as yours."

"I don't see you making any payments," she sarcastically said.

"There's no reason for either of us to make payments. The rent from the two apartments should be more than enough to make the payments."

"It might if I could keep them rented."

To keep from upsetting her more than she was, he didn't mention that if she had been a better landlord and maintained the apartments they would have stayed rented.

"And, by the way," she said. "Where's my $200.00 you said you would give me when you cashed Eddie's check?"

He had planned to give it to her, but had to say, "You told me to keep it."

"You wish!"

He handed her the money, and then told her everything Marcie had told him to say.

"You have eight hundred dollars?" she asked. "Four hundred for me and four hundred for the bank?"

"I'll have to borrow it, but I can have it by tomorrow." He didn't want her to know he had any money.

"Who's going to lend you that much money?"

"The bank, with Tom cosigning."

"It sounds to me like you and Tom have this all worked out, and I'm getting screwed."

"That's not true. The only involvement Tom has is cosigning my note. It's like this: if you don't take my offer and wait until the bank starts foreclosure proceedings, you'll wind up with nothing. But, if you accept my offer, we can go to the bank tomorrow, start the paperwork, and you'll get the four hundred. If you don't believe me, call Marcie."

"I'll call tomorrow. It's too late today."

"No, it isn't. It's only four, and Marcie's always there until five."

"All right, all right, I'll call, but I want to talk to her in private."

"That's fine. Jill and I'll wait outside."

They were barely outside when they noticed a small man, not much more than five feet, mowing Carl's mother's yard.

When he saw them, he turned off the mower and wiped the sweat off his face with the towel draped across his neck and shoulders.

"You must be Carl," he said while extending his hand. "And you must be Jill." Jill offered her hand and he grasped it in both of his. He pinched Tommie on the cheek. "And you have to be Tommie. You are a cute little thing, just like your grandmother said…. I guess you're wondering who I am. I'm Bart Fowler. I rent the little efficiency apartment in back from your mother. I work at night, and since I don't have much to do during the day, and love working in the yard, I keep Lois's grass mowed and whatever else needs doing."

"I was wondering who was keeping Mom's yard looking so nice. I knew she wasn't."

"She says she always kept a beautiful yard, and she wants to help, but, as you know, she hasn't been able to work outside since her last heat stroke. Your mother is such a fine person, and all she talks about is how proud she is of you and how wonderful Jill is and how cute and precious her granddaughter is."

Carl and Jill glanced at each other when Bart wasn't looking. They knew he had been conned.

Heat stroke! Mom's never been in the sun for more than thirty minutes in her life.

"You have her yard looking great. I'm sure Mom appreciates it."

"She does. I don't like to cook, so your mother cooks and I clean the dishes and kitchen."

"It seems to me that you and Mom have a good arrangement." Carl was smiling when he said, "Sounds like you and Mom might have a little something going."

"I'd like to, but you know your mother. She's extremely cautious about getting into a relationship. From what she says about the men in her life, the way they hurt and used her, I don't blame her."

He must have money.

Carl saw his mother standing behind the screened door. "Mom's off the phone," he said to Jill.

They told Bart it was nice meeting him, and then headed back to the house.

"According to Marcie," she began, "I don't have much choice. I told her what we agreed on, and she said she'll have the papers ready to sign the day after tomorrow."

"What time?" Carl asked.

"Two o'clock. I'll meet you there."
"We can pick you up."
"That's OK. I'll take my car. I want to do some shopping."
"Is anyone living in the house now?" Jill asked.
"No. It's vacant."
"Do you mind if we stop by and go through it?"
"It's yours and Carl's. Do what you like." She turned to Carl, "You still have your key, don't you?"
"I don't have one for the upstairs."
While glaring at him, she dropped the key in his open hand. "Enjoy your house."
"We will."

Carl and Jill had just started assessing the condition of their house when Ralph and Frances pulled up.
"I saw *Blue* and knew you were here. What's happening?"
"We now own my grandfather's house."
"It's about time," Ralph said. "What are you going to do with it?"
"Fix it up and rent it."
"Bobby's looking for a place to rent."
"You think he'd like to rent one of these?" Jill asked.
"He talked about how convenient it would be to live here next to Mom. But, he wasn't about to rent from Lois. He's coming to visit Mom in a little while. I'll ask him."
Frances held up her hand to show off her new ring.
"You're engaged!" Jill shouted.
"Yep."
They hugged. Carl shook Ralph's hand, hugged Frances, and congratulated them.
"When?" Jill asked
"We haven't set a date," Ralph answered. "She'll probably want a large wedding with all her friends, coworkers, and family."

"I do not!" She moved closer to Jill and Carl. "It was only yesterday when he proposed. We haven't discussed our wedding, but I can see we need to."

"You don't want a large wedding?" Ralph said.

"No. I want a wedding like Jill had. My family, your family, Carl and Jill, and someone to marry us. And I don't care who."

Ralph and Frances embraced. "That's what I'd like too," Ralph said.

"Now, when?" Jill asked.

Frances looked at Ralph. "You have two weeks left of your leave. How about this Saturday?"

After agreeing that Saturday was the perfect day, they, with Carl holding Tommie, began looking at the house.

"The furniture isn't bad," Jill said. "Like the rest of the house, all it needs is a good cleaning." When she looked at the bed in the master bedroom, she made a face as if she smelled something. "This bed has to go!"

"Guess we'll have to buy a new bed," Carl said. "The one in the other bedroom is probably no better."

They moved to the second bedroom, and as predicted, the bed was in bad condition.

"I have an idea," Frances said. "You buy a bed for the master bedroom; there's plenty of room in there for Tommie's crib; I'll bring my bed from home, and pay half of what you'd charge for rent, and," she looked at Jill, "you, Tommie, and I can live here. What do you think?"

Jill looked at Carl, smiled, then back to Frances. "I think that's a great idea."

"Sounds to me like we have some moving to do," Carl said to Ralph.

"This is going to work out fine," Ralph said. "Your wife and my wife living together, Bobby upstairs, and Mom next door. It can't get better than that."

The upstairs apartment was much cleaner, and the bed was in good condition. "At least," Jill said, "we won't have to buy but one bed."

Everyone agreed to start cleaning the next day. Frances would join them when she got off work.

The following morning, Carl stopped at the bank to give Marcie his $400.00 for the down payment—the four hundred his mother would receive.

"I thought it would take more than two days," he said.

"It normally does, but, I know how quick conditions can change with your mother, so I'll pull a few strings and rush it through."

"Will Tom need to be here?"

"He should, but if he has a charter for his boat, I'll give you the papers for him to sign, and you can bring them back."

"He does, but he's willing to cancel if necessary."

"We can handle it. There's no need for him to lose a day's work."

Except for his mother looking madder than a sett'n hen, the closing went well.

By the following Thursday, Carl, Jill, Ralph, and Frances had the house clean, a new bed, the yard mowed and trimmed, and all their belongings moved in. To celebrate, they went to the Snack House for dinner. Each waiter came to their booth to be introduced to Tommie. It was the first time they had seen her.

That night, Jill, Tommie, and Carl slept in his grandfather's home.

They moved Frances's bed in on Saturday morning. The wedding was planned for that evening. After their wedding, Ralph and Frances went someplace. They didn't tell anyone where. They returned on Monday and began living with Carl and Jill. Bobby moved upstairs soon after. It was the perfect arrangement.

Chapter 17

▼

Carl and Ralph finished their commitment to the Navy in July of '61. While in the Navy, Ralph had applied for a job with the US Postal Service. He was home for only a week when he was informed of an opening in Okeechobee. He accepted the offer, and he and Frances, reluctantly, moved. Carl and Jill had rather they stay, but were pleased that Ralph had acquired a job which not only had fabulous benefits, but the four years spent in the Navy would go toward his retirement.

During the last two years, Jill, Frances, and Tommie had become like family, and it was difficult for Jill and Tommie, especially Tommie, to watch their best friend pack and leave—it was just as difficult for Frances.

Carl was not anxious to find work. He wanted to spend time with Jill and get to know his daughter. But two weeks after returning home, the owner of the marina where he worked before moving to Naples, called and offered him a job. His old boss made him an offer too good to turn down. The owner had bought a sightseeing boat and while he operated it, taking passengers on cruises up the Caloosahatchee River, he wanted Carl to manage the marina.

One of the first changes to the marina Carl made when he took over was to become a dealer for Evinrude outboards and Woodson boats. Woodson Boat Company was one of the first boat manufactures to build fiberglass boats.

Using large letters, he painted the name of the marina on the sides of one of the boats, and on weekends, with his assistant manager running the marina, he, Jill, and Tommie cruised up and down the Caloosahatchee. They even took turns running the boat while the other skied. Mondays were always crowded with curious people.

Even though boats built of fiberglass had been on the market for a few years, his was the first marina in Fort Myers to sell them. Not only did the boat and outboard sales increase, so did water-skis, and all the paraphernalia that went with skiing. To keep up with sales, he became a dealer for several other boat manufacturers.

Three years later, when Tommie started school, Jill joined Carl at the marina, and it did not take long before she was selling as many boats, engines, and gear as Carl. Between the two, their income was substantial. But even so, after an additional six years, they became bored, and yearned to have their own sport fishing boat and charter business.

Since the death of his father, Carl and Butch had kept in touch. During one of their phone conversations, Butch asked Carl if he knew anyone who would be interested in buying his boat. Butch owned and operated a 42' charter boat.

Carl didn't hesitate. "Yes. I know someone."

"Who?"

"Jill and me."

"If you're serious, I'll make you a helluva deal."

"I'm definitely interested. But why do you want to sell?"

"My wife wants to do a little traveling and spend more time with our grandchildren. I never thought the day would come when I'd give in and admit it's time to retire…but I think it's time.

"My wife's been patient with me and my life on the water, now it's time for her to enjoy all the things she had to sacrifice so I could pursue my interest. She says we should tie an anchor to the hood of the car and start traveling the country, and when someone asks, 'What's that on your hood?' that's where we should settle down."

"Do you think you'll be content being away from salt water?"

"Probably not. But I owe it to Martha to try."

"Where, and when, can we see your boat?"

"I work out of Sarasota now, and she's docked at Marina Jacks. She's not chartered this Sunday."

"Sunday works for me."

Carl and Jill would normally drive *Blue* on weekends, but they were anxious to see Butch's boat. He felt comfortable driving their new car faster than he would *Blue*, so he chose to take it. He also preferred not to add to *Blue's* miles, even though it was only eighty miles to Sarasota.

By the excitement Jill displayed while driving to Sarasota, and after seeing Butch's boat, there was no doubt in Carl's mind that she was just as eager as he to get back on the water.

After Butch answered all their questions, and with Tommie right behind him, he climbed the ladder to the upper station. He fired up the engines and when they had warmed, he told Carl to cast off the lines, then headed for New Pass and out to the Gulf.

While Butch and Tommie were at the helm, Carl and Jill checked out the cabin and the rest of the boat.

"We have to have her," Jill said.

Carl was quick to agree.

Jill and Carl joined Tommie and Butch on the upper station. Tommie was at the helm. Butch was relaxing beside her. His hands were folded behind his head and his feet were propped on the console.

"Tommie's a natural," Butch said. "Look at our wake…. Straight as a string…. How old are you, Tommie?"

"I'm twelve."

"My goodness!"—Carl smiled; he knew the rest of what Butch was going to say; he had heard it many times when he was a young boy.— "When I was your age, I was only eleven."

Tommie and Jill laughed.

"Can we buy her, Dad?" Tommie asked without shifting her eyes from straight ahead.

"If we buy her, Butch," Carl asked, "would you consider running her until I get my captain's license?"

"I'll run her for as long as it takes. I'm not in a hurry to retire."

"It may take us a while to find a place in Sarasota to buy or rent, plus, we have to find someone to manage the marina."

"No need to hurry. I'm not going anywhere."

Carl looked at his daughter behind the wheel, then to his wife; her face reflected her desire. "We'll take her."

Butch stood, shook Carl's extended hand, then Jill's.

"The first thing in the morning, I'll call Marcie," Carl said. He and Jill thought the price Butch had quoted them earlier was extremely fair. "I'll write you a check for a deposit."

"I don't need a check. We have a deal. When you get your finances squared away, you can pay me then."

Carl would've preferred to work the boat out of Naples or Fort Myers Beach, but he knew there were no available boat slips.

"Are we going to keep the name, *Martha*?" Tommie asked when they left Butch and the marina.

"That's Butch's wife's name. Do you have another name you'd prefer?" Carl asked.

"Not really. I was just wondering."

"I hear it's bad luck to change a boat's name."

"Then *Martha* it is," Jill said.

Tommie agreed.

Since Marcie figured Carl was as good as any marine surveyor, and she knew Butch, she waived the customary survey and processed the loan.

Soon after notifying the owner of the marina of his intentions to leave and become a charter boat captain, an attorney approached Carl with an offer to buy his and Jill's home. They had been asked before, but had always refused. Realizing that downtown Fort Myers had engulfed them and the seclusion they had enjoyed was no longer, they accepted the attorney's offer. Most of the houses on Monroe Street, similar to his grandfather's, had been purchased and remodeled into professional offices. His grandfather's home was one of the last.

Carl and Jill no longer looked for a house to rent in Sarasota. They concentrated on finding one to purchase. They wanted to be sure *Blue* had a secure place to stay, so they only looked at houses with a two-car garage. Their realtor found the perfect house not far from Marina Jack's.

To move, it took two trips with the truck Carl rented. The first trip, Tommie rode with him in the truck while Jill followed in their new car. The second, Tommie rode with her mother in *Blue*.

* * * *

Tommie took advantage of every opportunity, summer vacation, holidays, and weekends, to help her dad with his charters, and by the time she was seventeen, she could maneuver *Martha* as good as any other captain could operate their boat.

Carl always acted as if he were busy and not paying attention to her or the people at Trader Jack's when, after a charter, Tommie backed into their berth. He would be, nonchalantly, scrubbing the cockpit and preparing the fish the customers caught for cleaning. Without exception, he waited until *Martha was* completely in and stopped before he removed the lines from the dock and secured her.

As soon as Tommie shut the engines down, and the roar of the large diesels subsided, and with everyone on the dock watching, she descended the ladder from the upper station, skipped the last step, and gave a little bounce when her feet hit the deck. Carl was always at the bottom of the ladder to hug and compliment her as if it were her first time.

The people on the dock would shake their heads in amazement. It was difficult for them to believe a girl weighing a little more than one hundred pounds could handle a boat that large. The same would happen when she pulled up to the gas and fuel dock for fuel.

Carl had told Tommie many times that she was just like her mother. He often thought how proud Tom must've been when, as teenagers, Jill or he, gently positioned his boat against a dock or backed it in its berth.

Carl was preparing his boat for an early morning charter. There were six in the party. Tommie had returned to school; it was her senior year. Jill usually helped him with a group that size, but she had other commitments. The thought of being alone, all day, with six inexperienced fishermen, had him concerned. The challenge of operating the boat while assisting the others had never been a problem. He had done it many times. But, for the last three months, during summer vacation, he had gotten used to Tommie running the boat while he helped the customers fish. He was going to miss her.

"Hi. Are you Captain Carl?"

Carl looked up and saw a young man standing on the dock. "Yes. I'm Captain Carl. Are you one of the guys who chartered my boat?"

"No. I'm looking for a job."

"Come aboard."

"Yesterday, when I asked the man in the marina's office if he knew someone needing a deck hand, he suggested you. He also said you were the best."

"What's your name?"

"Dan, Dan Allison," he said while offering his hand.

"Nice grip."

"You, too."

"Have you ever worked on a charter boat before?"

"No, I haven't, but from the time I was fourteen, during summer vacations, I've worked on my uncle's commercial fishing boat."

"How old are you?"

"I'm nineteen. I graduated last year. It seems strange not having to return to school."

Dan reminded Carl of the way he looked at nineteen, broad shoulders, a small waist, the same dark complexion, their height was even the same. The one thing that impressed Carl the most was the way Dan made eye contact while talking. He never looked away.

"Can you start today?"

"I sure can."

Once they were out in the gulf, Carl realized that Dan was more than a good worker. He was familiar with all phases of fishing and boat handling. He seemed to anticipate when the customers were about to experience a problem with their fishing equipment, or boarding a fish, and was there to help before they asked.

"What do you think?" Carl asked. "Is this something you want to do?"

"I love it! I hope you're pleased with my work."

"Very pleased."

"Good. I look forward to tomorrow."

"Me, too."

They were back at the dock and cleaning the boat when Carl saw Dan's mouth drop open and his eyes fix on something or someone on the dock. He turned to see what had gotten Dan's attention. It was Tommie.

"Hi, Dad."

"Come aboard. I want you to meet my new deck hand…. Tommie, this is Dan. Dan, this is my daughter, Tommie." He watched his daughter and Dan stare at each other for a moment without moving. Tommie was first to offer her hand.

Dan accepted her hand with both of his. "I'm glad to meet you."

"I'm glad to meet you too."

Even though neither smiled, Carl saw the attraction in their eyes. And, for a reason he didn't understand, he was pleased, not concerned.

"Whoa back!" Dan exclaimed to Tommie when he looked in the parking lot. "Is that your car?"

"No. It's Dad's. He bought her twenty years ago when he was only sixteen."

"She sure is a beauty. Do you drive it to school?"

"No. I'd never drive *Blue* to school."

"*Blue* must be her name?"

"Yes. The only reason I'm driving her today is because Mom had something to do and took her car. I thought Dad could use a hand cleaning the boat, but I guess I'm too late."

"We still need a hand to get fuel," Carl said while motioning toward the upper station.

Carl saw that Dan was impressed when he heard *Martha's* big diesels fire up then heard Tommie's command from the bridge, "Cast off the lines!" Carl watched Dan rush to untie the lines from the cleats, coil and place them neatly on the dock, and then the pilings when they passed. *He's a natural.*

Soon after Tommie eased *Martha* back in her berth, Jill stopped to see if Carl needed any help. She was on her way home.

Tommie introduced Dan to her mother.

"I've never seen a mother and daughter favor each other as much as you and Tommie," Dan said.

"Thanks. I'll take that as a compliment."

"It was meant to be."

"Well, aren't you the charmer."

He lowered his head and began to blush. "I better go below and clean the galley."

"I'll help you," Tommie said.

"I can't get over how much you resemble your mother," Carl and Jill heard him say. "But you have your father's eyes." Jill and Carl looked at each other and smiled when they didn't hear Tommie explain that Carl was not her biological father.

"Where did you find him?" Jill asked.

"He just walked up this morning and asked for a job."

"Did he do good?"

"He was great."

"He's definitely good-looking."

"It looks to me like Tommie thinks he is too," Carl said.

"I don't blame her. He reminds me of you when you were a teenager. How old is he?"

"Nineteen."

"That'll work."

"Now, Mom," Carl said, "let's not start making wedding plans."

She smiled. "He's just so damn handsome. I'd hate to see him get away."

Carl laughed and patted her on the fanny. "It's up to Tommie, and, as always, she'll make the right decision."

After a few weeks, Dan was able to handle *Martha* as good as Tommie. During the week, he was the one at the controls, but on the weekends the boat was chartered, which was almost every weekend, Tommie was in charge. He admired her ability and was never jealous.

While observing Tommie and Dan become close friends, Carl and Jill witnessed the same cautious behavior they had displayed while teenagers. They didn't want their daughter and Dan to feel uncomfortable with their blossoming friendship, so they chose to be discreet and not encourage or discourage them. They also agreed that if Dan and Tommie became more than friends, they would do their best to make them feel comfortable showing affection in their presence. They wished Jill's mother and Tom had done the same.

Chapter 18

As Jill and Carl predicted, Tommie and Dan became extremely close and spent every available moment together. Dan was Tommie's escort for her prom and sat with her family at her graduation.

"Will you be needing me when Tommie starts working full time?" Dan asked. Tommie had told him that she would be working with her father after graduating.

"I'll need you both," Carl answered. "In fact, I've been thinking about buying another boat, and if I do, I'll have to have a captain for her."

"You mean I'll work for the captain of the other boat and Tommie this one?"

"No. I want you to be the skipper of the newer boat. *Martha's* getting a little age on her, so I'll run her."

"Really! You want me to be captain?"

"Yes, I do. If that's what you want."

"Oh, it's what I want.... I've been studying. And it won't be long before I'm ready to take the test."

"How old do you have to be?"

"I thought it was twenty-one, but I called the Coast Guard and they said nineteen."

"That means I can buy a boat as soon as you pass your test.... I think the owner of the boat berthed next to *Martha* wants to sell. If so, the berth goes with the boat, and berths in a good location are hard to come by. I'll talk with him the next chance I get. But, no matter whether I buy a boat now or later, you have a job, Captain Dan."

"Captain Dan," Dan repeated. "Has a nice ring, doesn't it?"

"Yes, it does."

"Thanks, Captain Carl. I appreciate what you've done and what you're doing for me. I can't thank you enough."

Dan joined Tommie and her family for her eighteenth birthday—a week earlier, she was with him and his family at his home to celebrate his twentieth. While there, Dan approached Carl, "Captain Carl, I have a favor to ask."

"Sure," Carl answered. "What is it?"

"I've talked so much about your '47 Chevy to Mom and Dad that they'd love to see her. Would you mind if Tommie and I drove her over to my house?"

"I don't mind at all. In fact, you can drive her anytime you like. It'll do her good."

Dan thanked him, and Tommie said she would not be out late.

Carl heard the garage door open. He looked at the clock next to his and Jill's bed "Didn't Tommie say she'd be home early?"

Jill lifted her head, to see over him. It was 1:00 A M. "I hope they didn't have a problem with *Blue*," she said, and then put on her robe and went to check.

"Is everything OK?" Carl asked when she returned.

"She says they were just driving around. But, by her 'cat that ate the canary look,' I'm afraid *Blue's* 'sacrificial altar' has scored again."

"Please tell me you're kidding!"

"I'm afraid I'm not. I knew that someday it would happen. I'm just glad it was with someone who respects her."

"I can't allow myself to think about it. I don't want to admit that our little girl is no longer our little girl. It seems you're better prepared."

"For some reason, when they left tonight, I felt a girl was leaving, but a woman would return. I guess the reason I'm not surprised is because I'm aware of *Blue's* powers."

"I didn't know, while in school, you knew *Blue's* back seat was occasionally referred to as a sacrificial altar."

"Occasionally! Why, *Blue* and its back seat were the talk of the school. I heard several girls bragging to their friends about their exploits with you in your car. Hell, for some, saying they'd been laid in *Blue* was better than showing they were wearing your ring."

"You're exaggerating."

"Maybe a little, but don't worry, I wasn't jealous. At the time, I was proud to be a friend of the school stud. Later, I was just as proud to be his last. And," she leaned across him and kissed his lips, "that old stud is as good as ever—maybe better." Without saying another word, she began removing her gown, and he his shorts. After eighteen years of marriage, not once had either asked the other for sex. All it took was a touch, a look, a kiss, or an embrace. Their desire was always mutual, and often.

Carl had an early charter, so he and Tommie were having a quick breakfast before leaving.

"What did Dan's mom and dad think of *Blue*?"

"His dad loved her, we even took him for a ride, but his mother didn't seem to be impressed. She took a brief look, then said she had to do something in the house. I guess she's not impressed by old cars."

"Some people are like that.... We better hurry."

As soon as the two couples, one with a six-year-old son, boarded *Martha*, Carl sensed that he, Tommie, and Dan were in for a bad day. The kid paid no attention to his parents or the other couple when they screamed their demands, and they were constantly screaming. For the kid's safety, Carl knew he had to show his authority.

"Can I have your attention?" he demanded. They all gathered in the cockpit. He directed his comments to the kid, "I'm the Captain, and you need to understand that my orders are to be obeyed without question." He chose a small life jacket, then knelt down to the boy's level to help him put it on. "You'll wear this at all times," he didn't ask, he told.

"But, I don't want to! I don't like it." The kid squirmed away and rushed to the security of his mother's outstretched arms.

"Maybe," she began, "we can talk this nice man into letting you not wear it as long as the weather's good."

"Let me make something clear!" Carl felt his anger building. "To you, I can be called 'Man,' to your son, I'm 'Captain.' Now, he has to agree to wear this life jacket, and you have to agree to see that he does, or my boat will not leave the dock, and I'll refund your money.... So, what's it going to be?"

"We'll see that he keeps his life jacket on," the boy's father replied.

"Thanks. I'll put it on him and make sure it's properly adjusted." The kid agreed then cautiously approached. He had met his match in Captain Carl.

Except for the kid wildly running all over the boat, the day went surprisingly well. But as they prepared to return, the sky began to darken. Since there were no severe weather warnings on the radio before they left port, Carl figured it was just a normal summer squall and would last for only a few minutes. Tommie was running the boat from the upper station; Dan and Carl were busy stowing the fishing equipment and icing down the fish they caught, which were many. The wind strengthened, and Carl became concerned.

"Head her home Tommie!" Carl commanded, then turned to Dan, "Looks like it's going to be a bad one. Go forward and make sure the anchor is secured in its chocks. I'll check below."

Tommie chose a compass heading that would take them home, then turned *Martha* to the new heading.

Dan finished checking the anchor and joined Carl in the cockpit.

"Where's the kid?" Dan asked.

"I haven't seen him!" Carl shouted, trying to be heard above the wind.

"You didn't see him when you were below?" Dan yelled.

"No, I didn't! He wasn't with his parents! Maybe he's forward in one of the berths! I better go check."

"Are you OK?" Dan shouted up to Tommie. The wind was howling too loud for her to hear him. He cupped his hands around his mouth and shouted again, "Are you OK?"

"I'm fine!" she answered. "But I'm afraid I'm not going to be able to stay up here much longer! Look at how dark that front is! It'll be raining soon! Maybe we can outrun it!"

"I doubt it!" Dan shouted when he saw how fast the squall line was overtaking them.

Knowing Dan had finished checking the anchor and was back in the safety of the cockpit, Tommie pushed the throttles forward, and the additional speed caused the angle of *Martha's* deck to increase. From where she was, she could not see that the kid was stranded on the port deck, holding on for his life to the rail on the side of the cabin—Dan had returned on the starboard side after checking the anchor.

As Carl screamed to Dan that the kid was not below, a bolt of lightning struck so close that there was no pause before the deafening clap of thunder. Something caught Dan's eye as it fell overboard on the port side; he rushed to see what it was. It was the kid. Without hesitating, he dove in.

Carl grabbed the life ring from the port cabin side and threw it toward Dan, then yelled up to Tommie to stop the boat. She didn't hear him; her ears were still ringing from the thunder. When he realized she had not heard him, he bolted for the lower station, jerked back the throttles, and put the wheel in a hard port turn, but by the time the boat came to a stop, the kid and Dan were far behind.

"Where's my son!" his mother screamed when she came out of the cabin. "Where's my son?"

Carl was too busy to answer. He was fastening a strobe light to the other life ring. When he finished, he turned the light on and threw the life ring with the light attached as far as he could.

"What happened?" Tommie yelled over the kid's mother's screams and the wind. She had climbed down from the upper station.

"Dan and the kid are in the water!"

"They're in the water!" She looked aft, but the rain, which had moved closer to the boat, prevented her from seeing them.

"Yes! Now, listen to me!" He moved close so he wouldn't have to shout. "The most important thing we can do is not panic. The rain is almost on us so put on your foul-weather gear, then go back to the upper station. You'll see better from up there. Watch your compass and head in the opposite direction from what you were going. Go slow. We don't want to run over them."

From behind him, Carl heard the kid's mother screaming hysterically. He turned to see her beating on her husband's chest with her fist.

"It's your fault!" she shouted. "I didn't want to come and neither did he! You said we'd have fun and you'd watch him!"

Carl realized he had to calm her down before she said something that would never heal. He motioned for them to join him under the canopy, at the helm. He was holding *Martha* into the wind while Tommie dressed in her foul-weather gear.

"We'll find your son. I promise. He had his life jacket on and Dan is with him. So, please calm down. Now is not the time to blame each other. Now is the time to comfort one another. It may take awhile, but we'll find him. We just have to wait until this squall blows over." He continued, "There's nothing you can do to help, at least not now. So how about the four of you go below and stay dry. Tommie and I will take care of things out here. We'll be at the upper station where the visibility is better. I'll call you as soon as we see them."

The other couple helped the boy's parents below.

"Do you really think they're OK?" Tommie asked.

"I'm certain of it." He wasn't, but when he saw how what he said had lifted his daughter's spirits, he was glad he did.

"I'm ready to go up," Tommie said.

"Be careful. I'll be up as soon as I get my gear on."

She started for the ladder, but stopped, returned to her father and gave him a hug. "I love you, Dad."

"I love you too."

"I'll jiggle the wheel to let you know when I'm ready to take over," she yelled.

Carl had barely joined his daughter when the storm released a vicious punch. "I'll take her!" he shouted. "You watch for them! Your eyes are better than mine!" He ignored the compass and headed into the wind. "From now on we'll hold her close to the wind!"

The wind intensified until it was blowing the tops off the building waves. The rain had also increased, but now, instead of falling, the wind was blowing it parallel to the water. Soon the driving rain, mixed with salt water, felt like small shot or pebbles hitting their eyes, and they could no longer bear the pain of opening them. Shielding their eyes with their hands was little help. When they did manage a brief glance forward, they could not even see the bow of the boat. For relief, they had to lower their heads and turn their faces to the side. Carl looked to starboard and Tommie to port.

Under those harsh conditions, it was difficult for Carl to judge how fast or in what direction the wind was pushing Dan and the kid. He hoped his speed was not too fast and he had passed them, or too slow and they were far ahead. To add to his stress, the waves began to build. He knew with the additional wind, the waves would soon start breaking, and instead of Dan and the kid riding the waves, the waves would roll over them, which would be difficult to survive.

The wind and rain didn't start letting up until ten o'clock; Carl and Tommie had been on the bridge for seven hours. Their only breaks were when one of them went below to check on the boy's parents and the other couple.

Carl wished he didn't have to insist that his customers stay in the cabin. If he had allowed them to sit in the helm and companion seats under the canopy, they would've gotten wet but were less likely to get seasick, which they all were. But the risk of having someone else fall overboard was too great. Mostly, he felt sorry for the boy's parents all cooped up in the cabin, worrying about their son, and feeling helpless. That's why as soon as the wind and rain began to subside he informed them and their friends that it was clear enough to come out.

He instructed them on where to be: either on the seats, or between the seats and the bulkhead, but never aft of the seats.

"I see a flashing light!" Tommie yelled from the bridge.

"Stay right here and don't move." Carl commanded. "I'll let you know if it's them, and when you can help."

He took two steps at a time as he climbed the ladder to the bridge and upper station.

"Where?" he asked while still standing.

"Ahead and a little North."

He looked in the direction Tommie was pointing. "I'm pretty sure that's them; at least it's the strobe light. I hope they're with it."

"They will be," Tommie assured him. She was not going to allow herself to think anything different.

The night was extremely dark, which allowed the light to shine even brighter. He began panning the searchlight ahead, just in case Dan and the kid had not made it to the life ring with the strobe light.

The storm had stopped as fast as it began. Now they were left with the large waves that had not had time to subside. Many times during the night, he had thought of the night his father died, but now his father's death was heavy on his mind, and the closer they got, the more worried he became.

When the boat was close enough for the searchlight to make out what was there, he saw two life rings and two heads, but no movement. *Oh, my God!*

Tommie saw there was no movement. "Why isn't Dan waving?"

It was too dark to see her expression, but by the stress in her voice, Carl knew she was losing control.

"Their faces are out of the water, which is a good sign," Carl said. "They're probably too exhausted to wave.... I'm going down and attach a line to a life jacket, then I'll put the boarding ladder over the side. These waves are going to be our biggest problem, so don't try to get too close. When I think you're close enough, I'll throw them the life jacket and pull them to us. You can only help if you stay up here. So don't come down to help. OK?"

"OK."

If they were not alive, he didn't want her to be there when he brought them aboard.

"When you get close, turn off the bright searchlight, we don't want to blind them, then hold the flashlight on them."

"Is it them!" the boy's mother shouted when she saw Carl coming down the ladder.

"Yes, it's them."

The lump that was already in his throat became larger when he saw the mother's relief, and how she collapsed into her husband's arms. He turned on the cockpit lights, chose a life jacket, and tied a line to it. While putting the boarding ladder over the side, he heard both mother and father sobbing loudly. Not knowing what to expect, he didn't want to encourage or discourage them. Since he didn't know what to say, he didn't say anything.

As usual, Tommie's boat handling ability was outstanding; she maneuvered *Martha's* starboard side to within thirty feet of Dan and the boy. Carl threw the life jacket and it landed right beside them. When he saw that Dan didn't reach for it, he dove in. Tommie instructed the others to pull on the line when Carl made it to them and the life jacket.

Carl handed the limp, almost lifeless boy up to his parents. "Tommie!" he screamed. "Come down and help them!" Since she had attended the Red Cross life saving course, she would know what to do.

"Hello, Captain Carl," he heard Dan say as he approached him.

Carl lost control of his emotions, but managed to get out, "Hello, Captain Dan." With the boat rocking from side to side and Carl holding the ladder in one hand, he wrapped his free arm around Dan and pulled him close.

"Someone help me get Dan aboard!" he called out.

Dan was so weak, he could hardly move, but with the help of the other men, they managed to get him aboard.

Tommie was coming out of the cabin as the men were laying Dan on the cockpit floor. His smile caused her to lose control of her emotions, and she began to weep. With tears running down her cheeks, she rushed to him, pressed her body against his, and held him close. Carl almost wept too when he saw Dan's weak arms slowly raise to embrace her.

"How's the kid?" Dan asked.

"He's fine," she sobbed. "I took him below and covered him with blankets. His mother is lying with him to get him warm."

"I think you'd better do the same with Dan," Carl said. "As soon as I retrieve the life jacket and the two life rings, I'll head for home. I'll also call the Coast Guard and let them know we found them." He directed his comments to Dan, "They'll call your father and mother. I'm sure they're sick with worry."

"You called the Coast Guard?" the man, who was not the boy's father, asked.

"It was the first thing I did. I informed them of our situation and gave them our approximate location."

"Well, where are they?"

"They couldn't send their plane out in that weather and their boats were busy with other rescues. It was up to us."

The man helped Tommie with Dan while Carl finished securing the boat.

Chapter 19

It was two o'clock in the morning when Carl backed *Martha* into her berth. Jill was waiting on the dock. She jumped on board, attached a few lines to the cleats, but not all, then rushed up the ladder to embrace her husband.

"Where's Tommie and Dan?"

"Below."

"Are they OK?"

"They're fine. Exhausted, but fine."

As Carl secured the upper station, Jill hurried down to check on them.

"Look in the forward berth," Jill said when she joined her husband in the cockpit.

Carl approached the cabin door and looked in. Dan was on his back and Tommie, with an arm and a leg across him, was snuggled as close as possible. Both were sound asleep. The boy and his parents were also sleeping.

"What a picture," Carl said.

"I better go back in and check on the boy," Jill said.

Carl noticed the couple who were with the boy's parents, quietly standing in the cockpit.

"Are you still seasick?" he asked.

"No. We're just tired," the man answered.

"I think 'dazed' comes closer to describing our condition," the lady added.

The boy's parents, with him in his father's arms, joined their friends in the cockpit.

"Captain Carl's wife suggests we stop by the emergency room," the boy's mother said.

Her friends agreed.

Carl and Jill helped them off the boat and onto the dock, then watched as they ran to their cars. The friends waved, but the parents didn't even look back.

"They seem to be in shock," was all Carl said when he saw Jill's look of disbelief.

"Is Dan OK?" a man shouted while running from his car to the boat.

"Except for being extremely tired, he's doing good," Carl answered. "You must be his father?"

"Yes, I am. Where is he?"

"He's in the cabin," Carl answered.

Dan's father boarded the boat and started for the companionway, but stopped when he looked in and saw Dan and Tommie cuddled in the forward berth. Jill had left a light on.

"Are you sure he's all right?"

"I'm positive," Carl answered.

"Are you Captain Carl?"

"Yes." Carl said while offering his hand. "And this is Jill."

"I'm Al," he said as he vigorously, shook Carl's hand, then Jill's. "I've heard so much about you and Captain Carl. Tommie and her parents are all Dan talks about. I feel I already know you. You have to be extremely proud of Tommie. She's a wonderful girl."

"We are," Carl answered, "but I'm just as proud of Dan. If it hadn't been for his quick thinking and risking his life, the little boy who just left wouldn't be alive. Dan is a real hero."

"I wish his mother could be here to hear you say that. But, she can't. I admitted her in the hospital today," he looked at his watch, "I guess it was yesterday."

"I hope it's not serious," Jill said.

"No, nothing serious. She had her gallbladder removed. She had the surgery yesterday before the Coast Guard called.... I better hurry to the hospital and let her know Dan's OK. But I would like to talk to him before I leave."

"Hi, Dad. I thought I heard your voice." Al turned to see his son standing in the companionway. They embraced without talking. Jill and Carl knew that neither could.

When Tommie stepped from behind Dan, they all had a group hug, and a group cry.

"Are you Captain Carl Sanford?" The voice came from the dock.

"Yes. Who are you?"

"I'm a reporter. Can I ask you a few questions?"

"Please. Not now. We need to get home and rest."

"I understand. How about this afternoon, say about three?"

Carl put his arm around Dan and Tommie. "We'll be here."

Al shook Carl and Jill's hands before leaving for the hospital. Jill mentioned to Al that when his wife is well, they should get together for dinner. He agreed.

Carl, along with Tommie and Dan, was cleaning the boat when, at three o'clock, a man from the *Sarasota Herald-Tribune* came to take their picture. They were reluctant to pose, but he convinced them. When the photographer finished, Carl asked if the reporter he agreed to meet was coming. The man said he didn't think so. Carl was disappointed. He had made notes and was prepared to tell Dan's story of heroism. Later that day, Carl called and canceled those who had his boat chartered that week.

The following morning, when Carl opened his morning paper, he was shocked to see, right on the front page, the picture the photographer took. "Hey, Jill, Tommie. Come see what's on the front page of the paper!"

"Wow," Jill said. "What a nice picture of the three of you. And look at the size of the article. But you said the reporter didn't show."

"He didn't."

"Well who wrote it?"

Carl read the name to himself. "Well I'll be damned." He looked up at Tommie and asked, "Guess who wrote it?"

"I give up."

"The lady who was on board with us. The friend of the boy's parents. She must work for the paper."

With Tommie looking over one shoulder and Jill the other, they read the article. It was all there, accurate from start to finish and took up one third of the front page and half of the second. Tommie read out loud the writer's description of her father: "Captain Carl Sanford, a man who is as gentle as a kitten, but when he needs to be, he is as stern as a Navy Admiral. For instance: when we boarded his boat, *Martha*, my friend's son refused to wear his life jacket. Captain Carl insisted the boy wear it at all times, and then he ordered us to make sure he did. It was an order that saved the boy's life."

As expected, Dan was the hero, but since he was in the water most of the time, the majority of the article focused on the relentless wind, the heavy rain, the enormous waves, and Captain Carl and Tommie's ability to hold *Martha* close to Dan and her friend's son. Since the writer was cooped up in the cabin during the worst of the storm, she didn't elaborate on what happened outside. But, Jill, Tommie, and Carl felt her pain when they read her account of how difficult it had been for those in the cabin. She also expressed admiration for Tommie's endurance, her compassion, and her boat handling skills.

"Well," Jill said when they finished reading, "I guess you guys are the local heroes. You better prepare to be interviewed by the media."

"That's the last thing I want," Carl said.

"Come on, Dad," Tommie pleaded. "We owe it to Dan."

"You're right. Everyone should know he risked his life to save that kid."

As soon as he finished the sentence, the phone rang. Tommie answered it. It was Dan. She and Dan talked about the article for a while, then he mentioned that his mother had called from the hospital to let him know how proud she was.

"She also asked me to ask your father if he would mind stopping by the hospital sometime this morning."

Tommie relayed the message. Carl didn't understand why Dan's mother wanted to see him, but agreed with Jill that he should go.

"Tell Dan to tell his mother I'll be there before lunch. And ask him for her room number."

Carl read the sign: Visiting hours: 2:00 to 4:00 P.M. and 6:00 to 8:00 P.M. He wondered why Dan's mother had asked to see him in the morning. Since it was not time for visiting hours to begin, he walked by the lady at the information desk and went straight to her room.

Before entering the room, he looked in. Lying on the bed, looking toward him, was an exceptionally attractive lady. He stepped back and read the number again.

"Hi. Are you Dan's mother?"

"Yes. Come in." Her face reflected pleasure.

"I'm Carl."

"I know."

He thought she must've recognized him from the picture in the paper. His eyes were fixed on hers while he waited for her to introduce herself. The long pause caused him to feel uneasy.

Without moving her eyes from his, she began to smile. "You don't recognize me, do you?"

Where have I seen her? Her eyes, her smile, and her voice, they're all familiar. "I'm sorry," he said while staring at her beautiful face and eyes, "I don't…. Give me a clue."

"Let's name her *Blue*."

"Eve!"

"Yes," she said while lifting her arms, inviting his embrace.

Being considerate of her operation, he supported most of his weight on his elbows while they hugged. When he began to lift his chest from hers, he felt her gripping his shirt, preventing him from pulling away. While leaning over her, and looking at the tears in her beautiful, blue eyes, he said, "I've thought of you many times since that night."

Even though her eyes were filled with tears, they remained fixed on his. "There hasn't been a day I haven't thought about you." Her hands released his shirt and her arms slowly slid from his back as he straightened up.

"Why would you think of me?"

She lifted her hands to her face and wiped the tears from her eyes before answering. "I think of you each time I look into your eyes."

"What do you mean, 'each time you look into my eyes?'"

"Your son has your eyes."

"My son.... Dan is my son?"

"Yes. Can't you see the resemblance?"

"I have to sit." He pulled a chair close to her bed.

"Well, can't you?" she asked.

"See the resemblance?"

She nodded.

He noticed her chin trembling. He leaned toward her, reached for her hand, then held it with both of his. "From the first day he came aboard my boat.... When I look at him, it's like looking at a reflection of me when I was his age. Jill, my wife, says he even walks like me."

"He doesn't walk. He struts."

"That's what Jill said, but I didn't want to say that.... Does he know?"

"No. By the time I decided to tell him, it was too late, he and Al were close and it would've broken his heart. Al knew when we got married that I was pregnant with someone else's child, but he loved me and looked forward to being a father. He's been a good husband and a great father and I love him very much."

"Does Al know I'm Dan's biological father?"

"No.... Hell, I didn't even know until Dan and Tommie brought *Blue* over to show us."

"Is that why you didn't go for a ride?"

"Yes. After seeing *Blue*, I became so nervous, I had to go inside. I was also shocked when I discovered that after all these years, I didn't know your last name. I thought it was Danford. That's why our son's name is Dan. I also realized I had to tell you."

"I'm glad you told me, but what made you think you had to tell me?"

"You see how much in love Dan and Tommie are. I'm worried to death that it won't be long before they start making wedding plans. And then what can we do? We have to do something now."

The more Carl listened, the more his smile increased.

"Why are you smiling?" Eve calmly asked.

"There's nothing to worry about."

"How can you say that?...They're brother and sister!"

"No, they're not. Tommie is not my daughter. At least not my biological daughter."

"Oh, Carl.... You're being honest with me." She squeezed his hand. "Right?"

"Yes. I wouldn't kid you about something this serious."

"You have no idea how relieved I am to hear that.... I've had one helluva week. I started the week wondering if I should tell you, and when I decided to, I worried about how to tell you...that's probably the reason my gallbladder flared up...then I had to have surgery. On top of all that, Dan, Tommie, and you were caught in that storm. What started off as the worst week of my life has turned out to be my best."

"There's nothing more I'd like than for Dan to know he's my son, but I'll never tell. If he's told, it'll have to be you."

"I'll give it some thought."

Carl was silent for a moment. "But," he began, "I have to let my wife know. We don't keep secrets from each other, and if I tried, she'd know I was hiding something. Honesty has been a big part of our marriage, and I think she deserves to know. If you knew Jill, you'd realize that she's going to be just as pleased as I am to know Dan is my son. And, she won't resent you in any way, and your secret will be as safe with her as it is with me. The last thing she'd want is to create a problem for you, Dan, and Al. Trust me. Telling Jill will be much better than not."

"I understand. It's like the obligation I felt to tell Al I was pregnant. My only regret is that I never told Dan."

"I'm pleased that you understand."

"I do.... Now I'm anxious to meet Jill. She sounds like an exceptional person."

"She is. You'll like her, and she'll like you."

Eve paused for a moment. "I just have to ask. Do you ever think about that night?"

"Many, many times, and I'm sure there'll be many more. Not only did you name *Blue* that night, that's the night I lost my virginity."

"I knew you were, but you sure as hell didn't act like a virgin."

"Have you ever thought about that night?"

"Have I!…I still wake up in the middle of the night thinking about it. As I told you, you were my third, but I didn't tell you that you were the best. I planned to tell you when you returned."

"You can't believe how much I wanted to see you again, but…"

"I know. Bobby told me…. I think it would be best if we changed the subject."

"I agree…. You cut your hair!"

"Yes. I also gained a lot of weight. That's probably the reason you didn't recognize me."

"You don't look heavy to me."

"I'm a lot heavier than I was the night we christened *Blue*."

Carl raised her hand to his lips and kissed it. "I guess it wasn't a safe time."

She smiled. "It was the right time."

"I thought we were going to change the subject."

"God knows I'm trying."

Carl smiled and patted her hand. "What did you think of the article in the paper?"

"It was fabulous. But if it was as bad as she wrote, it's a wonder any of you survived."

"It was bad."

"I'm so proud of Dan."

"Me, too. If it wasn't for him, that kid wouldn't be alive. Not only is he a hero, he's a wonderful person. You and Al did a good job."

"I think it's in his genes."

He stood, leaned over her, and kissed her lightly on the lips. "Thanks, Mom, for a terrific son."

"We did good. Didn't we?"

"Yes we did."

He placed the chair back against the wall, then returned and stood by her bed. For a while, they could only look at each other and smile.

"I guess," he said, "the next time I see you will be at Dan and Tommie's wedding. If they choose to marry."

"I'll see you at their wedding."

Chapter 20

As Jill predicted, Dan, Tommie, and Carl were asked to be interviewed many times; they accepted all. Dan and Tommie were even on a TV morning show in Tampa. A limo picked them up for that.

Not long after their lives got back to normal, Carl purchased the boat next to his. Now, *Martha* and the new boat were berthed side by side. Dan passed his test, and became a licensed charter boat captain. Carl paid a sizable down payment for the boat, and Marcie's son, who was now the president of the Lee County Bank, financed the remainder.

Also, as predicted, Tommie and Dan became engaged.

The new boat needed some major repairs before Carl and Dan felt comfortable chartering it. So, between charters aboard *Martha*, and when they returned from a charter, Dan and Tommie stayed busy cleaning and repairing it. A few days before their wedding, she was shipshape and ready to go.

Dan and Tommie were standing on the dock, admiring the results of their hard work, when Carl joined them.

"Are you going to leave the name?" he asked.

Tommie answered, "Even though you say it's bad luck to change the name, *I Catch'em* has to go."

"What are you going to name her?"

"We decided to name her after Dan's mother."

"Eve?"

"No. Evelyn."

"How did you know Mom was once called Eve? I've only heard her friends from long ago, call her Eve."

"I don't know. I guess I just assumed you'd shorten it to Eve."

"You don't like the name, *Evelyn*?" Tommie asked.

"I think it's a wonderful name, and I like it much better than Eve.... I don't know what I was thinking."

Tommie and Dan preferred to keep their wedding small. Captain Butch and his wife, and the lady who wrote the article in the *Sarasota Herald-Tribune* and her husband were the only invited guests. The others were family: Dan's parents; Tommie's parents and grandparents: Tom and Joyce, and Lois and Bart.

Carl was not as reluctant as he would have been, about ten years before, to have his mother attend Tommie's wedding. She and Bart had married and both stopped drinking. They had to. When his mother drank, she became mean, sarcastic, and belligerent; Bart became mean and, even though he was small, enjoyed a good fight. And, he was stubborn enough to not leave when she tried to throw him out. They were still living in Donnie's house.

Bart loved to fish, so two or three times a year, Carl, Tommie, and Jill took him and Carl's mother fishing. Carl and Jill were amazed at how his mother had changed from a person they were uncomfortable being with to someone they enjoyed. Tommie treasured her time with Granny Lois and Pappy Bart, as she called them.

The wedding was held in Jill and Carl's home. When Carl introduced Evelyn and Al to Jill, he was careful to not make the mistake of calling her Eve. Evelyn's tension was obvious, but quickly changed when Jill approached with open arms. As they hugged, Evelyn looked over Jill's shoulder at Carl and smiled, and by the length of their hug, especially when they hugged again, Carl knew Evelyn was aware that he had told Jill. When Jill embraced Al, Evelyn and Carl embraced.

"I'm glad you told her," Evelyn whispered.

During the ceremony, Jill saw Carl and Evelyn glance at each other and smile.

"You and Evelyn have to be so proud."

"I'm sure she is. I know I am. But, the one I'm most proud of is you. Thanks for understanding."

Jill and Evelyn stayed close for the rest of the evening.

The day before the wedding, Carl and Jill, without Dan and Tommie knowing, had the old name on the new boat removed and the new name, "Evelyn," painted on the hull and life rings. That night, they informed Dan and Tommie that for a wedding present, they were giving them the down payment portion of the boat. All they had to do was make the payments and the boat was theirs.

Knowing their granddaughter and Dan owned a charter boat, Tom and Joyce's wedding present was enough fishing equipment to get started. For Dan and Tommie's wedding night, Al and Evelyn provided the wedding suite at the finest hotel on Longboat Key.

Through the years, Tommie had heard about her mother and father's first anniversary at Little Marco Island aboard her grandfather's boat, and for her honeymoon, she wanted to cruise to the same place on her and Dan's boat. The morning after their wedding night, Al, Evelyn, Jill, and Carl met them at their boat to see them off.

"I see you painted the new name on," Tommie said to her parents.

"What do you think of our boat's name?" Dan asked his mother.

"I don't know. What is it?"

Carl and Jill put their arms around each other and watched Evelyn's eyes fill with tears when Dan pointed to one of the life rings. She struggled to speak, but couldn't.

The newlyweds had stocked their boat with enough supplies to last a month, even though they planned to be gone for only a week. All that was left to do was fire up the large diesel engines and cast off. When the engines warmed and the instruments checked out, Tommie threw the lines to her dad and said, "Thank you, Mom and Dad, and Al and Evelyn, we'll see you in a week," then climbed the ladder to the upper station to join her husband.

The parents waved without talking as *Evelyn* eased out of her berth.

Before *Evelyn* was out of the marina, Dan's mother said, "What a beautiful way to start a marriage."

"Yes, it is," Jill answered.

Al and Evelyn left soon after the boat was out of the marina. Carl and Jill stayed.

With their arms around each other, they watched the newlyweds turn into the channel, and when smoke billowed up from *Evelyn's* exhaust and her bow began to rise, Jill said, "She's not our little girl any longer."

"No, she's not," Carl said as they tightened their embrace.

"Tommie is so lucky…. She'll always be happy."

"I hope so."

"She will."

"How do you know?"

"She found someone exactly like her father."

"Dan will be happy too," Carl said. "She's just like you."

Jill pressed her head against Carl's shoulder; *Evelyn* was out of sight, and had been for several minutes. "Do you know what I'd like to do?"

He didn't take his eyes off where he had last seen his daughter and Dan. "No, I don't. But I'm sure I'll like it."

"Since their first stop is the Fort Myers Yacht Basin, and they'll be staying overnight there, let's drive down and watch them arrive."

"We can't do that," Carl said. "They'll think we're worried and checking to see if they made it."

"I don't want them to see us."

"They can't see us from our special place."

She turned to face him. "I know."

By her smile and the sparkle in her eyes, he sensed she knew what he was going to say.

"Let's take *Blue*."

FROM THE AUTHOR

I have been asked many times if *Nights Remembered* is based on my life—some of it is, but most of it isn't. I was twelve years old when my father died in an automobile accident, the same age as Carl; my mother cheated on my father, the same as Carl's; and I did make a trip to Punta Gorda. Unless you have read, or plan to read *My Brother's Mother*, you will just have to wonder which other episodes I experienced.

Before I wrote *Nights Remembered*, I wrote *My Brother's Mother*, a memoir. In it, I describe how difficult my brother and my lives were while being raised by a mother who was less than desirable. I often wonder why I wrote the story; I think it was more for healing than any other reason—and it helped. Her story also inspired *Nights Remembered*.

I thought no one would believe *My Brother's Mother*, so I chose to write a fictitious story and use some of the experiences I was forced to endure while living with my mother. I had no idea that *Nights Remembered* would generate the many questions it has, especially, in Southwest Florida. To answer their questions, I print them a copy of *My Brother's Mother* and send it to them. Some have gone to the trouble and expense of getting copies made for their friends and relatives. I can't believe the number of letters, and phone calls, I have received—all advising me to get it published.

Not long ago, my mother passed away, and I made the decision to put her story with the other memorabilia I have for my children and grandchildren. But, after hearing from those who read it, I am convinced that, as it helped me, it could help someone who is struggling to deal with a self-centered, alcoholic parent or spouse.

Now that Mom has passed on, I have to change it from present tense to past tense, and as soon as I finish, it will be published.

978-0-595-35996-7
0-595-35996-5